I0623899

THE BOARDWALK

RYAN J. PELTON

COMMON GRACE PUBLISHING

This is a work of fiction. All the characters, organizations, locations, and events portrayed in this novel are either product's of the author's imagination or are used fictitiously.

The Boardwalk © Copyright 2017 by Ryan J. Pelton

All rights reserved.

Second Edition

ISBN-13 (Print): 978-1-949420-07-4

Published by Common Grace Publishing

Learn more: https://www.ryanjpelton.com/common-grace-publishing

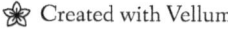 Created with Vellum

THE BOARDWALK

I see nothing in space as promising as the view from a Ferris wheel.

   -E.B. White

JULY 1, 2016

I don't know if anyone will ever read this journal. My therapist thought it be a good idea to write my struggles with The Cancer. I wish I had a clever name for it, but I know it sucks. When you get to my age, most people get it, whatever it is.

I'm not much of writer, and not very reflective these days. If words scrambled and incoherent blame the chemotherapy. Kid's, maybe you'll find something entertaining, tell your own rug rats around a table during Thanksgiving dinner. One can hope.

That's how I'd like to imagine it before I can only pee through a tube.

People tell me to have hope. The doctors are confident we can beat this thing, whatever this thing is. Not sure how they know because the Big Guy in the Sky is in control of when I checkout. I want to go peacefully and quietly. My friend William got The Cancer and had to shit in a bag. I hope it doesn't get to that point.

You get older and see the twists and turns of life. Relationships shipwrecked, promises broken, fulfillments and joys, and everything in between.

Like when you were born, Sherry. The nurses gasped when they saw your chubby body in the delivery room. I'll never forget that day.

One day I laid on the therapist couch and she challenged me to write about a significant event during my sixty-five years of life. She said there's power in getting shit out in the open, my paraphrase.

Oh, how I know.

When you live long, there are many experiences that make top of the list. But, one experience in particular will always rise to the top. Something I have never shared, at least not until now.

The summer of 1979 changed everything.

Details blur with passing of time. I'll do my best getting the meaty parts right.

'79 is when I danced between high school and college trying to find a place in the world. The 70's were still a fun time in America when the pace felt right. Cars we're manlier, Facebook was not a thing, Netflix binging was thirty years away, and the Internet didn't waste years of our lives.

We lived in a small beach town in California called "Oceanside." The post World War Two boom of suburbia and economic flourishing was waning in the midst of an oil crisis and impending housing market crash of the 80's. That's what caused your mom and I to move to Texas in 1986.

The Boardwalk on the shores of Sea Lion Beach was an attempt to fight the struggling tides of a community that was no longer a destination. A place to have fun, spend money, and hang out. I got a job working The Snack Shack and wanted to kill myself most days.

But, the summer of '79 forever etched in the deep recesses of my mind. I met a girl, Sherry, which you'll hear more about later. You now understand sweetie where your name came from. Sorry if I never told you.

Sherry was a good thing. Despite her confusing signals, I wanted to marry her, which I thought was God's plan, or at least my plan.

Meeting Sherry led to some dark stuff, things I've never talked about and still don't know what to think. Not even my therapist knows. I think it explains a lot of how my life turned out.

I don't know if what happened in the summer of 1979 ruined my life. Still, it led me down a path riddled with regrets, three wives being one. Well, here's my story, the best I can tell it. I know little and have little wisdom to offer. But, whoever will read this story remember one thing: Be careful on the Ferris wheel.

IN THE SUMMER OF 1979, The Boardwalk became the battleground of young hearts at Sea Lion Beach. Mine included. Pause long enough and I can smell the nacho cheese sauce that introduced me to the love of my life.

Our small crew of love-hungry, hormone-ridden teenage boys, with incomplete mustaches, and short list of dates experienced the coldness of rejection amidst the warm California sun. My anthem Thomas Petty's "I Need to Know" spinning on repeat for most of the summer.

I'd do anything to have Sherry Lewis. Even if it killed me. That's not hyperbole or clever metaphor. I needed to know if Sherry Lewis was into me. Never could tell. She had that flirty personality, where you didn't know if you'd be making out later at the Twin, or watching her brother's baseball game at Heritage Park *as friends*.

The cheese sauce dripping from my elbows, down the side of my white Ocean Pacific shorts and onto the floor of The Snack Shack, was not helping the cause.

I didn't see her that day. But, I could smell her. A lavender perfume tickled my nose, or maybe it was shampoo, not sure. Thirty years is a blink and a blur when hair is now growing in wrong places and fighting the same insecurities originating on the shores of Sea Lion Beach. It felt like yesterday when I announced to the world my woman problems. Not much has changed, just ask my three ex-wives.

On that Friday in August, what I call "S-Day," I cobbled together coherent words that would at least make me appear datable. My confidence shattered when a reflection off a napkin dispenser revealed a volcanic crater forming on the bridge of my nose. A common summer occurrence caused by the elixir of daily sweat and sunscreen.

An angelic voice spoke from behind the greasy counter of the Shack, "It looks like you're having trouble with that cheese pump." Sherry leaned over the counter and handing me a pile of napkins.

I gave a glance in her direction and almost stopped breathing. At least that's how I remember it. Sherry's face was unblemished from pimples and scarring unlike my own.

I thanked her for the napkins and wondered how to be cool sliding a pool of fake yellow cheese off my right leg onto the floor. I cupped another clump of cheese with my hands as it poured over the sides of the napkins. "If this damn thing...," I said, glancing up to see if Sherry had already run away screaming down the beach. I tilted my head to the left and didn't make eye contact in hopes she didn't see the pimple crater, "If this damn thing... jams up, I meant to say, jams up again...," I mumbled.

Any semblance of coolness pooled up on the cheese soaked concrete floor of The Snack Shack. The summer job from hell.

"If you give an extra pump in between servings, it won't jam," Sherry said, with a smile revealing a dimple on her right cheek.

"What?"

"If you give an..."

"I heard you. What do you know about food service?"

"I wouldn't call cheese dispensed from a pump 'actual food.'"

"True," I replied, and wiped my cheese drenched hands with a towel.

"Used to be in food services. I made nachos for my little brother's Little League team in Long Beach. The cheese pump jammed all the time until I used that trick. One pump, maybe two, and you're back in business. We all took turns at the snack bar. Kinda like this one," she said, staring up at the large red, blue, and yellow letters of THE SNACK SHACK.

The sunset exploded behind the wooden pier in the distance as August drew closer to September. You could hear the faint shouts of kids riding the Ferris wheel and bells ringing at the Strongest Man game. Development of The Boardwalk, or "TB" as we called it, transformed Oceanside into a hang out, and not just a resting stop for homeless hippies. The suits believed the renovated attraction would rival Coney Island on the east coast. TB the powerhouse of the West.

A swift beach breeze swept through the Shack and a pile of napkins leapt onto my cheese covered leg. Sherry leaned over the counter and covered a small laugh with one hand and peeled back a couple layers of paper mush with the other.

Oh, the hands. Strong, and yet soft, and tender like she'd never worked in her life.

I threw up my hands in surrender and watched Sherry clean me up. "Summer can't be over soon enough. I can't wait for this shit-hole to close down so I can get on with my life," I said.

Sherry glided to the right side of the Shack, reached over the half door, and unlatched the lock. She waved me in her direction as I hesitated not sure what she wanted. There were no cusThomasers, but I didn't want to leave the Nacho post. "I don't know what life you have to get back to. We need to fix you up, though. Come with me cheese boy."

She yanked my arm toward her and my feet almost left the earth. "You can't work the rest of your shift looking like a nacho monster threw up on you," she said, dragging me to a bank of outdoor showers. They lined a long bike path weaving between the sand and shops on the hill of Sea Lion Beach.

"What do you think you're doing?" I asked, staring up at the metal nozzle of the shower.

She jammed her soft hands against a round nob hanging on a pipe, "You got extra shorts?"

I nodded yes.

"We will end the cheese escapades. There's places cheese isn't meant to live."

I flinched with the initial hit of the water on my crotch and fantasized Sherry in her bathing suit joining me for a swim in the ocean. We were laughing, hugging, and doing other stuff kids do who are in love; use your imagination.

I placed my hands over my shorts like the scene when Marilyn Monroe's skirt blew up from a city grate. Not my greatest moment of the summer.

But, moments and dreams were all I had. Nothing happened during the summer of '79, well, at least not with Sherry Lewis. I had nothing going for me beyond the Shack. Maybe general education credits at Oceanside Community College in the fall. Tickets to Fleetwood Mac in a couple weeks with my friends. The night ending with drinking too much and talking about all the girls we could've had. High school was in the rearview mirror and I didn't know what to do with my life. But, the one thing I wanted, Sherry, didn't see what she was missing. Hard to see through all the cheese.

Sherry released her hand from the knob on the shower and stood back like looking at a Mona Lisa, "Not bad young man, not bad. I think we tamed the cheese monster. Go get those shorts and you're good as new."

I wrapped my arms to my chest and tried to fight off the cool of the approaching evening. I examined my cheese-less legs and clothes and realized that pimple. And, my nipples now poking through my wet white Snack Shack t-shirt, "Thanks for the shower, but I rarely shower on the first date."

I couldn't believe a coherent line came out of my mouth. It felt confident and lacked insecurity. Like maybe how the jocks in high school talked to girls. Not normal for me then, or ever.

"I don't even know your name," I said.

She reached out her hand, "Sherry Lewis."

"Neil Gordon."

Sherry gave a half smile, "You doing anything after your food services shift?" she asked, knowing full well what I served to beachgoers wasn't food.

"Nope, no plans for the rest of my life."

"That doesn't sound right for a working man like yourself. Probably have many audacious plans and goals for the future."

I stared back at the Shack which represented the first eighteen years of life. Not much to show for it other than soggy clothes and incompetence in how to work the cheese sauce dispenser in a four dollar an hour job. "The only plans I have are to close up the Shack and take you on the Ferris wheel," I offered, pointing at The Boardwalk.

Sherry glanced at the ground and acted like she didn't hear my invitation. She played with her nails. I waited for rejection common for most invitations to the opposite sex.

"Can we do something else?"

"Why, you scared of the Ferris wheel?" I asked, giving her a bump on her arm.

Sherry didn't look up and tried to avoid the question. "Not, exactly. I'd just rather do something else, cool?"

"Okay... Star Wars is playing at the Twin. Why don't I go home, change, and meet you there at eight?"

Sherry seemed relieved at the new plan, "Yes, that'll be great, see ya at eight."

I watched Sherry disappear into a sea of vacationers and locals hanging onto the last shades of summer. I was no different. But, one thing was certain. I needed a job that didn't involve cheese sauce.

I STARED at the bathroom mirror and couldn't avoid the giant pimple growing like Mount Vesuvius center stage on my nose. I clicked opened my mother's powder container and looked around the bathroom pretending spy cameras might find me out.

Sammy Baugh let me in on a pimple trick senior year. A dab of mother's makeup can take the redness out and keep you in the game. At least minimize staring and pointing until the swelling subsides. Most of the teenage years is pimple management.

I dabbed.

I wished the bathroom routine was an isolated incident during the high school years. Pimples, no. Dates, yes.

Unless you count Samantha Potter who was more of a stalking situation. I'd stare at her in Geography class and she'd turn away, roll her eyes, and pop a pink bubble of gum in disgust. I thought it was flirting. She wanted a restraining order.

I'm not sure why the ladies showed little interest. Nice guy that didn't have a record. Didn't look like a total monster, unless you counted the pimple monster on my nose. I get pimples, but doesn't everyone? Still getting them at sixty-five.

Sherry Lewis showed interest in a kind of *I'm never going to tell you how I feel* way. The conversations filled with hints and innuendoes of liking me and never coming out and saying it, riddled language like a Russian spy using code diverting an enemy. A brush of the hand, fluttering eyelashes, and petite kiss on the cheek. Come on, what does this mean, already?

She saw the pimple and still wanted to hang out. Didn't that mean something?

My long blonde hair neglected most of the summer. Arrested it down with water and slapped a pile of Dippity-Do gel in the palm. Made a pass getting fingers tangled in the mess fighting off tears. I winked at the mirror.

No Burt Reynolds, but not a monster, either.

I headed to the bedroom, sprayed cologne in the air, and danced through the mist. Another Sammy Baugh trick. My dad called it foofoo juice it for job interviews and weddings. Dad believed smelly guys never got jobs or found wives. He had both.

Don't know if I wore cologne for the Snack Shack interview, but I was gainfully employed and needed a date, before a wife.

Turned off the turntable playing Fleetwood Mac's "Don't Stop" and headed to the car.

I drove a white 1969 El Camino with a 405 V8 and wide tires. My dad and I spent the summer of '78 rebuilding the engine. I think that was when he shared sage wisdom on cologne and finding a wife. Something about working on cars brought me and dad together. I don't remember all the advice he gave, but he was a good dad. Always present. I miss him every day.

The El Camino rumbled in the driveway, and I listened with pride as I gave a little more gas. I gave a couple more revs and glanced to the neighbor sipping a beer in the window. We both gave thumbs up, kind of a guy bonding thing over muscle cars. If you're a lady you might not understand.

Mr. Higginbotham moved to the porch and rocked on a swing raising his Schmidt's. It was an evening ritual after the death of his wife. Married fifty years. I couldn't fathom loving someone that long. I wanted to date someone that lasted longer than a gallon of milk. Maybe Sherry would be the one? Tonight would be a good start.

I squealed out of the driveway and enjoyed the warm California wind blowing through my gelled hair. I prayed my pimple concealer would hold before Sherry changed her mind.

The Oceanside Twin sat on the end of Main Street and was always packed on a Friday night. With only two screens it never had much selection and the closest theater was in Bayside, about 30 miles away.

A flickering of lights lined each side of Main Street. Ed's Diner sat on the right, the best milkshake in town. Mario's Pizza, on the left, made a meatball sandwich straight from heaven. Cleaners, shoe repair, and Zody's Grocery, provided most of everything you needed in this beach town. Oceanside was big enough to have things to do and small enough to be annoying. Everyone knew who you took to prom.

The Twin was in front of me, as I veered to the right, and looked for parking along the street. The butterflies in my sThomasach were a signal altering me to a foundational truth. I had little experience dating girls. What do I say? Do I pay? Do I hold her hand? How's my breath? All the unknowns swirled in my head and I lost track of the parking search.

My last kiss happened at an 8th grade party where we played Truth or Dare. I got dared, and kissed Katie Williams, the largest girl in our class. The closet smelled like my grandmother's mothballs and Katie's breath smelled like onions. Not a memory worth reliving or replaying tonight.

The El Camino rumbled down a side street passing dozens of cars. Heads turned when I punched the gas. A man holding a girl's hand slipped off the curb. I bobbed my head side to side looking for parking.

Butterflies flooded my insides when I thought about Sherry, her smile, hands, and smell. She had a certain *it* about her. A kind of sweetness with an edge. I didn't know why she drew me in that day at The Shack, and every day that summer. Her sweet smile, exotic smell, and the way her eyes, oh the eyes, melted my soul. I wanted to run. Maybe vomit.

I found a spot in front of a green trash bin behind the Twin. I gave one last glance into my rearview mirror and puffed into a hand. Breath check.

Nothing to worry about. It's a first date, right?

I gave a pep-talk, like running out of the tunnel on a Friday Night football game. I was the kicker on our school's team. You'd think it might help with the woman woes. Yet no, it made it worse. I can still hear the comments: "Why don't you play other positions? Do you know how to tackle?"

I glided around the corner from behind the theater and headed down the sidewalk to the ticket window. I suddenly knew of how I walked and kept looking down wondering if it looked smooth. Convinced myself the walk caused the problems of a dateless existence.

A marquee in red letters read "Star Wars: New Hope."

The Twin was playing a rerun of the first Star Wars hoping to get publicity for a second installment. I pulled up my sleeve, checked a watch, and adjusted my butterfly collar. I was ten minutes early.

My dad programmed in me early. Being late not acceptable. Equivalent of being a serial killer. He'd say, "Son, what if there's a massive accident on the highway or you get a flat tire? Give yourself plenty of time in case President Carter launches World War Three and you need to find an empty bomb shelter."

Taking dad's advice meant a lot of standing around and waiting. No World War Three, yet.

A young kid wearing a Star Wars t-shirt leaned against a wall in front of the theater. I slid over to him and gave a smile, "Can I have a smoke?"

He handed me an unfiltered Camel, and I jammed it in my mouth letting it dangle at the corner. I only smoked when nervous. "Can I get a light?"

The kid looked me up and down and blew smoke to the side, "First date?"

"Shit. You can tell. What does a first date look like?"

"You."

"Dammit. Anything I can do to look less first-date-ish?"

"For starters, zip up your pants."

I turned to the side and hoped no one was looking at my crotch. "Jerk. My pants are zipped."

"That's a test. You wear first date all over your face like that pimple you're trying to hide."

I almost fell on the ground with panic. "You're kidding, right?"

"I know the concealer trick. You didn't do a great job. Gotta cake that stuff on like painting a house. That pimple be shining red before the opening credits."

I took a drag and could feel my armpits getting wet. "This isn't going well. I like a girl. She's smoking good looking, and I want to make a good first impression."

"Relax, love machine."

"What other sage advice you got, Yoda?"

"That's it... relax. Be yourself. That's all you can do, man. If she doesn't like you for you, tell her to screw off."

I nodded and smoked and took in the sage advice from the skinny Star Wars nerd, "That makes sense. Be me. Relax. I got this..."

"That's how I get chicks. You gotta show them who's in charge. Make them beg for more. Works like a charm."

I gave a look up and down at the nerd and couldn't conceive of any woman rolling around in his Star Wars bed sheets. "I noticed you're alone and wearing a Star Wars t-shirt with a Wookie on it. Where's the chicks you speak of?" I asked, giving him a smile, and blowing smoke to the side.

"How do you know I didn't make out with a chick before I came tonight? Maybe she's in the car freshening up after we did it in the backseat? You don't know me."

"Sure, you're right. Anything's possible. I could be way off about you and the ladies."

I tossed my cigarette on the ground and took another look at my watch. It was eight o'clock. "Thanks for the cigarette and advice. I'm sure it will work like a charm. I will keep an eye out for my date," I said, giving the kid a handshake. He nodded and disappeared inside the theater.

I paced the lines of people and kept an eye out for

Sherry. I thought of all the reasons she might be late. *She wanted to look extra good for me tonight and bought a new dress. A flat tire. Maybe World War Three?*

My father would be appalled.

8:10, then 8:20, then 8:45, then 9:30. I leaned under the sign of a square marquee of Star Wars and looked at my watch one more time.

Sherry didn't show.

The movie let, out and a swarm of people and voices herded around me. I felt a hit on my shoulder and looked up to see the Star Wars nerd. "Where's your date, in the bathroom?"

I stared at a piece of gum on the sidewalk. I didn't make eye contact with the nerd feeling like the gum. Crushed. Dirty. My breath now smelled bad.

"Not, exactly. She's a no-show."

"Oh, shit," he said, sliding down to sit next to me on the sidewalk. "Maybe she got a flat tire. Shit happens, you know?"

I knew Sherry was out of my league and had second thoughts of dating a pimple-faced kid serving nachos to beachgoers for minimum wage.

"I don't think so. This is a pattern for me," I said to the nerd.

He slugged me in the arm and rose to his feet. "Don't worry man. They're more fish in the sea. Screw her, she's missing out on a good guy."

"You don't even know me."

"Well, you were taking her to the best film of all time. You have fine taste in cinema. Means something in my book."

I gave a half smile and didn't want to talk about it

anymore. "It doesn't mean much if you have to watch movies alone."

"Remember, relax, be yourself. You'll be fine."

"Thanks."

I drove down Main Street and the sea breeze of Sea Lion Beach calmed my anger for a time. I thought a life of celibacy and singleness was in the cards. Glanced at rearview mirror and glimpsed the red pimple smiling back at me.

"Damn. I don't want to watch movies alone the rest of my life."

THE NEXT MORNING, I swirled my Frosted Flakes watching them get soggy in a Star Wars bowl. Residue of gel stuck in my nest of hair with one side standing straight up.

My sister Kim came up behind me and smacked the back of my head, "Nice hair, retard."

I ignored the assault, a daily occurrence with the younger sister. Kim was two years behind me in school and on a mission to ensure she was queen bee of the home. My mother and father bought into her manipulation and showed grace upon grace. If they only knew what she'd done when they weren't falling for her games.

Like dating Owen Mercer the ultimate Oceanside man whore. Owen was twenty-one and didn't mind dating a sixteen-year-old sophomore. Kim wasn't his first or last. He shacked up with every girl in high school. Never adjusting to life outside Oceanside High, he was the living cliche of football team captain, Chevy Camaro driving, man muscles... and no pimples. He still attended football games three years removed from Oceanside and stalked innocent young girls, like my sister.

"What did you do last night?" I asked.

"Hung out with Susie."

"Susie, or your man whore, Owen?"

"He's not a man whore," Kim cried.

I set my spoon in the bowl of cereal as Kim slouched down in a chair next to me. "What happened?" I asked, not all that concerned. Maybe if my parents saw me being nice, they'd pay for gas once in a while.

Kim grabbed a napkin from the center of the dining room table and dabbed her tears. Residue of black mascara from the night before surrounded each eye. "We were at a movie last night, making out... I mean, eating popcorn, and things are going great. Suddenly, and out of nowhere, Owen leans over and says, 'this ain't going to work out.' Right in the middle of kissing... I mean eating popcorn. He leaves me at the theater. Asshole just walks out, and I call Susie for a ride."

"I'm no *Dear Abby*, but what'd you think would happen? Owen's dated every girl in Oceanside county between the ages of sixteen and twenty-one. Twice over. You're just another pawn in his man-whore game of chess."

Kim trembled and ramped up her crying, "Owen was different. We had that chemistry, like Barbra Streisand and Robert Redford in *The Way We Were*. I thought he might be the one."

I held back laughter and tried not to say something making me a total dick hole. "Sorry, don't watch chick movies. I bet the chemistry was amazing. At least Owen showed up."

"Is this one of your weird jokes? The ones you have to explain. What do you mean?"

"Got stood up last night."

Kim wiped face clean, her tears subsiding, to give a

moment of attention. I could tell she didn't care all that much and found my pain amusing. She propped her head off the table with her hands. "Whoa, this is huge, big bro. Tell me more. You haven't had a date since... I don't know... when?"

"Dating dry spell, yes. But, I'm pickier than you. I don't date any Homo Sapien with a pulse."

My sister slugged me in the arm and rolled her eyes. "Go to hell. Owen was my soulmate. I'm no whore, bro."

Took my cereal bowl to the sink, and bit my lip not to laugh at the soulmate comment. "You're no whore. Just don't know how to be alone. How many guys have you dated since freshmen year, like twelve? I'm alone all the time... you should try it."

"Ha, ha dickwad. Tell me about the chick that stood you up. Is she real, or fake, like the girl you made up for an entire semester senior year?"

Molly Maddox was a girl at a rival high school. She was captain of the cheerleading squad, school class President, blonde bomb shell, and into me for me. Except, none of it was true. Tired of people asking who I was taking to prom. We went to her prom instead.

"Sherry Lewis is a real person. One of the most beautiful girls I've ever met. She came to The Shack yesterday, and we fell in love."

"It must've been love at first sight, or fright, because she didn't make it an entire day. Where'd she ghost you?"

"The Twin."

"*Love at First Bite*?" Kim asked.

"*Star Wars*."

"There's your problem. You don't take a first date to *Star Wars*. You take them to a Dracula spoof, like *Love at First*

Bite. Star Wars is for nerds. You need to show a different side, Neil."

"Well, it didn't matter. Looks like neither of us got bit by love last night."

My mother glided into the kitchen wearing a blue bath robe and rubbing her eyes, "What are you kids arguing about?"

"Oh, you know, teenager stuff. The finer things of cinema and love," I said, giving Mom a hug.

Kim looked in my direction and without words turned on the waterworks. Mom glanced up from making a cup of coffee and saw Kim welling up, "What's wrong honey?" she said, rushing over and wrapping arms around her neck.

"Susie and I got in a huge fight last night."

"Susie Gardner?"

"I don't think we're best friends anymore."

Mom picked Kim up from the chair and pressed her blonde ponytails against her breasts, "Tell your momma what happened?"

"It started at the Twin. We couldn't decide if we wanted to see Star Wars or Love at First Bite. She wanted Star Wars, and I wanted First Bite. I told her Star Wars is for nerds, joking. Susie called me a bitch and left me at the curb."

I hopped on the counter, crossed my arms, and watched the theatrics unfold in front of my sleepy eyes. Caught a glimpse of Kim smiling through her tearful face planted in Mom's bosom.

I mouthed "you asshole."

"Doesn't sound like something Susie would do. Over a movie? You girls always find compromise."

"I know, right? A movie? She's changed. I don't even know who she is anymore. The love gone..."

I didn't care to watch any longer and butted into the conversation, "Mom... I got stood up on a date last night."

My mother glanced up from holding Kim to her chest and gave me a puzzled look. Like she couldn't believe I had the audacity to speak amidst my manipulative sister.

"Not now, Neil. Can't you see your sister is hurting. You can be so selfish sometimes."

I smiled conceding Kim had won the game. It didn't matter if I was abducted and raped by aliens. Mom and Dad loved my sister more. They say parents aren't supposed to choose a favorite kid. I guess there are exceptions to every rule.

"Stood up by the most beautiful girl in Oceanside. I'm hurting real bad today, oh so bad," I said, in a monotone voice knowing no one cared, or was listening.

I jumped back to the floor and poured a glass of water from the tap. "Why don't you ask Kim why she's a liar? Who she was really with last night?"

Mom pushed Kim back a couple inches from her chest and glanced in my direction, "What did you say, Neil?"

"Ask Kim... who she was with last night. Susie, or someone, oh I don't know, more man-like?"

Kim's eyebrow shot up and waited to see my next move.

"Are you accusing your sister of lying? If she said she was with Susie, I believe her. Unless there's something she needs to tell me," Mom inquired, peeking down at Kim who was making sobbing sounds, "Were you with Susie last night, or not?"

"Neil's a prick. He doesn't understand the pain of love and losing a friend. The love Susie and I shared is gone and all he can do is accuse me of being a liar. You're right Mom, he's selfish. He's just mad a girl stood him up. Very mature... Neil." Kim tried to hold back a laugh.

Mom shook her head in disgust like I revealed being a serial killer or molesting babies. Kim's games didn't phase me anymore, and it was more fun getting a rise out of her, than anything. I think it's a way siblings cope in the pain of the teenage years. Whoever said high school would be awesome is ridiculous. Our relationship is still good today despite Kim being the favorite.

"Don't listen to your brother. He doesn't understand love. He's a man," Mom declared, rolling her eyes and shooting out a hip.

I said nothing.

Kim wiped down her tears, and Mom refilled her now cold coffee. Mom's countenance changed to a look of fear and seriousness, "Kids, there's something I need to tell you. Sit down, please..." she said, ushering us to the dining room table.

"Love's a hard thing. It's tricky, as you both know. And sometimes love fades with passing of time. People fall out of love and it's hard to understand the complexity..." she said, staring into the botThomas of her "#1 Wife" coffee mug.

"What is it Mom? Is everything okay?" I asked.

She paused, and glanced to a window at the side of the dining room, and locked eyes on a bird sitting on a limb. She wouldn't look us in the eyes, "Your father and I are getting a divorce."

I DIDN'T KNOW many kids with divorced parents. There was Richard Baxter in fourth grade whose parents split. But his father slept in another room of the house until Rich graduated. Does that count?

Divorced people existed but were ignored and taboo depending on the circles in which you ran. My folks were not churched people but divorce seemed foreign, like the California Angels winning the World Series. I thought nothing would tear them apart. They had a Kryptonite averse marriage no evil genius could break down. Everything seemed good with my folks on the surface. I guess closed doors tell a different story.

A warm breeze landed on the outdoor patio of Sea Lion Beach. A seagull picked at a fallen French fry as bikers, walkers, and skateboarders dodged one another on a cement path between beach and restaurants. I leaned back in my metal chair and people-watched and waited for Larry to arrive.

If anything could bring me out of the disastrous ending to summer of '79, it was Rathan's. You might've heard of

Nathan's Hot Dogs in Coney Island, New York (more popular for hot dog eating contests today). This was the poor man's California version, and not as good I'm told.

The founder of the rival hot dog chain of the West Coast was an entrepreneur from Texas, Bill Hicks. He believed Sea Lion Beach could rival the Coney Islands of the world. Rathan's would be "hot dogs with heart." Don't know what that meant. The only heart was heartburn coming in the middle of the night, especially if you ordered the AThomasic Dog, a foot long with chili, jalapenos, and drenched in cheese sauce. Bill was also the brains behind redeveloping the Oceanside community with The Board-walk, another attempt to rival Coney Island and similar such attractions.

Larry shook the back of my leaning chair and I had a mini-heart attack.

"What's happening loser? You order any food, yet?"

I shook my head and examined the clothes Larry was wearing, "Did Stevie Wonder dress you this morning?"

"Oh Neil, my unstylish friend. You're obviously not in tune with 1979. An amateur fashionista would know these are the threads of the modern age."

Larry Appleton was my best friend from life's first cry. We lived on the same street and attended the same schools until graduation day only a few months earlier. Larry wanted to be a film director and prized himself on being in the know with the latest pop culture and fashion trends. The problem is no one ever had the heart to tell him most of his trend-seeking made him look like an idiot.

I massaged Larry's sleeve with the back of my hand and gave him a smile, "What's this made of? Silk?"

"No, my silly friend. It's silk's second cousin, polyester.

I won't lie, it's hot as shit. Hot as Oceanside in the middle of summer," Larry said, wiping his brow of sweat.

"I'm not sure the girls will be attracted to your sweaty running suit."

Larry slouched down into a chair, rolled up his sleeves, and reached for a menu. "I might've underestimated the warmth of the day and polyester doesn't breathe much. But this... to be precise... is no running suit. It's a track suit. The track suit of the future."

"You don't run."

"True. But, when the ladies see a dude wearing this Puma track suit the panties will fly off. Kind of like Dustin Hoffman at the movie premiere of *Kramer Versus Kramer*, I'm told," Larry said while examining red, white, and blue stripes on the shoulders of the track suit.

Larry talked like he had insider information about movies and movie stars. It was only from reading endless pop culture and film critic magazines.

I shook my head and scanned the outdoor patio of Rathan's expecting all eyes to be on Larry's ridiculous outfit. The waitress came up and took our orders. Larry gave a nod thinking this short, cute, brown-haired girl was into him.

"You look hot in that thing," she said.

"What do you mean by... hot?" Larry asked.

She pulled out a pencil that rested on her ear and poked at Larry's side, "You got sweat stains on your running suit, hon," she said, snapping her gum.

"It's not a running... never mind. I'll take a Rathan's Special with a Coke."

"Same," I said.

The waitress popped a bubble of her gum and walked away giggling in the distance.

"She seemed into you," I said, caressing his polyester sleeve.

"Shut up a-hole. Trendsetters and geniuses were always misunderstood in their generation. Van Gogh never sold a painting when he was alive."

"'Van Gogh' said the man in the sweaty track suit. I'm not sure genius is your problem. Pit stains scared her off."

Larry lifted his arm and swiped it with a finger and smelled it, "Not good."

There were never times when Larry didn't make me laugh. More often because of his crazy ideas and what he deemed fashionable. Regardless, he was the loyal friend you needed when the botThomas fell out. I was feeling a little better just watching his idiocy unfold on the patio of Rathan's.

"Speaking of panties falling off. How'd the big date go Friday night?" Larry asked.

I tried to avoid the question and change the subject. "Ugh, it was fine. You think Nolan Ryan will have a good year for the Angels?"

Larry gave me puzzled eyes, "Like fine, we ended up in the back of your El Camino, fine?"

"You're such a whore. Is that all dating is to you? I don't kiss and tell."

"Neil, I've known you for eighteen years. Let's stop the shenanigans. You didn't even get to first base, did ya?"

A benefit of a lifelong friend is they can you read your mind. The curse... they can read your mind and know when you're lying. I never could get one past Larry, even if I tried.

"Not even a foul ball," I said.

"That bad, huh?"

"She was a no-show."

The waitress came back to the table with our plates of

dogs and Cokes. She paused and took another look at Larry and snickered. He held up his hand, "I get it, you don't like my threads. But, let me ask you a question," Larry said.

I slouched in the chair and tried to hide my face from what Larry might do.

"What do you think of my friend here? You'd date him, right?"

The cute waitress took a look over and gave me a thumbs up, "Thanks, babe. My friend got stood up Friday night and needed that to bolster his confidence with the ladies. You can go now," Larry said, as he waved her away like a King sending back food. The waitress rolled her eyes and disappeared inside.

I slugged Larry in the arm and tried not to yell and scare the other cusThomasers, "You're such a dick hole. You didn't need to do that. I don't need a confidence booster. I'm good with the ladies."

Larry was right, though. I wanted to end up in the back of my El Camino with Sherry, or anyone. I needed a confidence booster and didn't have a clue what to do with the ladies.

In Larry's unorthodox ways of showing it, he had a good heart. He had my back and wanted things to go well for me.

"When was your last date before Friday?" Larry asked.

"Don't keep track. It doesn't matter. I'm fine. Things are chaotic and having a girlfriend will just add to the noise. It's a blessing in disguise that Sherry didn't show up at the Twin."

"What chaos? You work a shitty job, might attend Community College in the fall, and have tickets to Fleetwood Mac in a couple weeks. Not exactly the inspiring life of *Brian's Song.*"

Larry was right, not on fashion but on a lot of things. He

knew I was insecure and often gave me a kick in the pants when needed. I could've got into an Ivy with my grades but was afraid to be on the opposite coast. Larry even helped with the application.

"I don't want to rush into anything and regret the decision," I said, picking at my fries.

"Like going to Harvard? Asking that waitress out? You can't live like this man. Go after stuff. Don't be scared to fall on your face."

"Like you?"

"Who else sweats his ass off to look cool on a hot summer day? Who makes movies in his backyard and sends them to Stanley Kubrick for review? And, who asked out the prettiest girl in school over the loud speaker during halftime of the basketball game? Me!"

That's the difference between Larry and I. He didn't give a shit about what people thought of him or if he failed. I cared so much that it froze me. I didn't want to move the chess pieces of my life in fear one wrong move would ruin everything. And... he sent a movie to Kubrick, and the halftime thing is real. Big balls.

"You're right. I need to take more risks in life. Just not right now."

Larry finished the last bite of his Rathan's Special. He wiped mustard from the corner of his mouth and gave a belch, "Stop being a pussy. Don't let the best years of your life pass you by. Ask the waitress out when she brings the bill."

"What? No way. I said I don't want to date right now. Things are hectic."

"What is so hectic? Please explain..."

"Parents are getting divorced. My mind is still processing it."

Larry set his Coke on the table and removed his Elvis-looking large rimmed glasses, "What the hell?"

"Mom told me and Kim this morning."

"That's heavy. Is your dad getting tail on the side?"

I spit an ice cube at Larry, "I don't know, dick. It didn't come up. We know little."

Larry waved the waitress over who was standing at the outdoor register. She came up to the table, "Can I get the bill? I'm paying today. My comrade's wounded and needs a pick-me-up. Will you take this handsome man on a date to cheer him up?"

My face turned four different versions of red and I slumped back in the seat, "Please ignore my sweaty friend. I'm kind of in a relationship, no hard feelings."

Before the waitress could respond another woman's voice came from behind our table.

"In a relationship? I hope it's with me," said a red-headed girl wearing Daisy Dukes.

Larry looked at me and then looked at the red-headed girl and shrugged, "Larry, this is Sherry. Sherry, this is Larry."

The waitress vanished with Larry's money and I wanted to vanish from the earth.

I EXCUSED Larry and his sweaty track suit, wanting no extra distractions. Larry wouldn't help with the cause to get a date with Sherry. He doesn't do serious. Only if it involves critiquing the latest film playing at the *Twin*.

I thought walking along the beach would be safe for necessary yelling. I wanted to yell. Maybe scream. Not because Sherry stood me up, that happened a lot in my dating career. I had an unusual callous built up over my heart that didn't allow heartbreak to become a mortal wound.

Still, I wanted another shot with Sherry. It was my parents where I felt the callous separate. That's where the screaming was bubbled up.

I paced along the shore with Sherry, not knowing where to put my hands. After being stood up I assumed hand holding presumptuous. Sherry held sandals and splashed her toes in the water as it washed up next to us. I glanced at her perfect ankles. Oh, the ankles.

I used a stick as a cane and slapped at sand and rocks. Sherry broke the silence, "Um, where to begin?" she asked.

Played it cool and acted like I didn't know what she was referring to. I tried humor to ease the tension in the salty air, "Start at age one and work your way to the present. Sound good?"

Sherry swung a sandal I dodged it like a bull fighter, "Last night, stupid."

"Oh, that. No worries. I bet you had a good excuse for breaking my heart," I said, with a wink.

Low tide turned high, and the water raced further up the beach. We laughed and scampered up the embankment trying not to get soaked. We found a dry spot higher up on the sand. "I'm sorry about last night. The truth is... I don't have an excuse. I was scared."

I held the walking stick on my head and smiled, "I'd be scared, too. Meet a guy working in a glorified snack bar. You shower him, see his nipples, and then he asks you out. Terrifying. How'd you know he's not Son of Sam?"

Sherry enjoyed my sarcastic humor and gave a sweet laugh. Her laugh turned back to serious, "There's always the risk of dating a serial killer. Relationships haven't been good of late."

I slung the walking stick into the water and nodded in agreement. "I knew we had something in common."

"Did you break up with a boyfriend not too long ago?" Sherry covered her mouth, "I mean girlfriend?"

I found her misstep funny and plopped down on the sand gazing into the vast Pacific Ocean, "My last boyfriend was the worst. He was sooo mean," I said in my best Valley Girl imitation.

Sherry giggled.

"To be honest, I've had little luck with boys or girls most of my life."

Sherry stood akimbo, staring down on me, with her feet

buried in the sand. "That's surprising, Neil. A guy who knows the finer things of cheese sauce distribution and holds a steady job. I'd think girls and boys would knock down The Snack Shack daily."

Summer of '79 led me to believe love wasn't for me. An endless pursuit leading only to frustration and pain. Maybe the callous over my heart needed guarding. I needed to seal it off. The news of my parents' divorce gave little hope. But love is love. It's a faucet that never shuts off. Ask my three ex-wives. Love drew me to Sherry that summer, or that's what I told myself. I wanted her to love me back. I wanted her in my life despite all the mixed signals. Love is risky, like Mom said. I wanted to risk. Why else be this persistent after getting ghosted at a movie?

Love.

"You'd think gainful employment would be a chick magnet, not so much. And, if you recall, we met when I was covered in nacho cheese sauce. I'm *no* Romeo."

Sherry threw herself down next to me on the sand and snuggled in close. I could smell her perfume or shampoo, I never could tell. It melted me, and whatever she said next didn't matter. Lost in all things Sherry.

"I'm scared. My last boyfriend was a loser. He treated me like shit."

"You want me to rough him up," I said, punching a fist into my hand.

"That's unnecessary. Besides, you'll probably run into him sooner or later."

"What do you mean?"

"He works at The Boardwalk. He's around Sea Lion Beach all the time."

"That'll be awkward. What does he do?"

"Sea Lion Flyer... maybe Dante's Hell. It doesn't matter."

I'd kill to get a job running rides on The Boardwalk. Beats dishing out nachos to ungrateful kids on family vacation.

Bill Hick's dream was to make The Boardwalk an amusement park destination, a rival to Coney Island of Brooklyn and Seaside Heights in New Jersey. But, it was too expensive to pull off in California. He didn't have the land space, and existing beach housing limited what he could do at Sea Lion Beach. He'd have to settle for a glorified carnival with better rides.

"You think the *ex* can get me a job?"

Sherry looked at me like I called her fat. "Talk about awkward. What if things work out with us? You don't think it's weird asking him for a job? Besides, I don't want to talk with him right now" she said, her face turning to a scowl, and tossed a shell into the rising tide.

It was those comments that kept me scratching my head for most of the summer. You want to be my girlfriend or not? She ditches me on a date and is worried about me running into her ex-boyfriend. You see what I mean, mixed signals.

"I heard the ride runners get paid double what I make at the Shack. My last raise was a quarter and that ain't going to pay for college or gas this fall."

It was true. Bill Hicks philosophy was to pay his workers at The Boardwalk well in hopes they'd stick around all year. Happy employees equaled loyalty in his mind.

"College man. What are you studying?"

"English. I'm going to be a writer."

Sherry slugged me in the arm and lit up, "Ooh... I might date the next Hemingway?"

"Maybe, but Hemingway's a hack. I never understood the love affair with him. *The Sun Also Rises*? Come on."

"Nooo... you're kidding, right? The love story between Jake Barnes and Lady Brett? One of the best books ever. His prose is like butter. What's not to love?"

"Butter? You're brainwashed like the rest. We we're forced to read him in high school like every kid in America. English teachers paid to make you think classics are *really* classics."

Sherry nodded and played with sand between her toes. I could tell she had something on her mind. "Neil, I need to tell you something. There's more to my past I think's important before anything happens...," she said, focusing on getting the words right.

"After the Hemingway comment nothing will surprise me," I said, with a half grin.

"I was in a serious relationship. That's why I ditched the movie."

"I know. You told me. Loser guy, works at TB. Too soon to date?" I asked.

"Not exactly. There's more. I met Kelvin at The Boardwalk."

I tossed a handful of sand on Sherry's toes and smiled in a playful way, "Oh, I see. This is your thing. You pick up hot guys along Sea Lion Beach."

Sherry grinned, "No, sir. I met Kelvin while working at The Boardwalk."

I could tell Sherry didn't want to dig any deeper into the conversation. She stared down the beach and made minimal eye contact. Not sure what the big deal of working at The Boardwalk was, except making more money than me.

I probed further.

"Okay, what's up? Did you play the ghoul who walks along the pier and scares kids?"

"All I can say is something bad happened, and I got fired."

I wiped sand from my hands and looked at her puzzled, "Who cares? Everyone gets fired. I lost a lifeguard job last summer because I let my friends bring in beer after-hours. Welcome to the club."

Sherry rubbed her soft hands along the sand and drew a smiley face with a shell. She took a deep breath, "I got fired because..."

Sherry paused. An eruption of tears and sobbing ensued.

I leaned over and placed an awkward hand on her bare leg, "It's okay. You don't have to say anymore."

A tear slid down Sherry's cheek and she wiped it away, "It wasn't my fault, Neil. It was an accident. I didn't do it. You don't understand..."

I wrapped an arm around her side and pulled her in, "I believe you. No need to explain. Don't beat yourself up... accidents happen... I'm sure there's a rational explanation."

When I sat with Sherry on the shore that August evening, she could've told me she was pregnant with an alien. It wouldn't of mattered. I wanted to be in her life in a bad way. Didn't know all the details of the firing and it sounded harmless. I'd find out sooner or later.

Sherry leapt to her feet like she was bitten by a crab. "I better go. I've said too much. You're probably confused, aren't you?" she asked.

I paused a couple beats and thought about my next move. "Girls thrive in the game of confusion. I would ask you out again, if you're up for it."

Sherry slapped my arm with my confusing girl

comment and looked surprised and glanced at the beach floor avoiding the question. "I don't know, Neil. You seem like a great guy. Never opened up like this before. But my wounds are fresh, if you know what I mean."

I reached into the back pocket of my shorts and yanked out a wallet. I handed Sherry a card. She read it. "Neil Gordon. Head of Food Services. The Snack Shack. You have business cards?"

"Don't ask."

I ripped the card from her hand. "I'll make it easy. Let's have a do-over. You call me at this number in the next forty-eight hours. If I don't hear from, no harm, no foul. We'll always have the shower and a walk on the beach. But if you call me, we go out, and I pick the place. No pressure. Nothing weird. And I promise no Ferris wheel."

Sherry wagged her finger and smiled, "Funny. This was kind of like a first date, you know?"

"Okay... I'll take what I can get. Let's try for a second."

Sherry tucked the card into a back pocket in her tight Daisy Dukes and gave me a hug. "Thanks for letting me spill my guts tonight. I'll tell you more later."

"Sounds like a date?"

"If you're lucky."

Damn. You see what I mean. I never know what she's thinking.

Forty-eight hours came and went. I didn't expect otherwise, but it would've been nice to gotten a call, telling me I'm hideous and not date-worthy. Something. Anything.

I had another issue to figure out that summer. I needed a new job because The Snack Shack was closing for the season. Got wind The Boardwalk was hiring employees for the off-season. I needed money to pay for college and gas. Match made in heaven.

The advantage of TB being on the West Coast is the weather. They could stay open year-round even when the Pacific ocean became cold from October to April. Cold water, yes. But, air temperature never fluctuated twenty degrees most of the year. The summer crowds didn't compare to the rest of the year. But, Hicks still made money year round. Win for the West Coast.

I stood on the pier examining my application, scanning for spelling errors. Bill Hicks the owner and founder of the theme park interviewed all new employees. He believed in the product and didn't want unmotivated teenagers, and adults, screwing up his empire.

When I called TB office to set up interview a sweet old woman, I think Hicks' wife, told me to meet him by the Ferris wheel. I didn't know where exactly, but 9 AM was the time. I was early.

Hicks was an eccentric man who didn't like doing business based on the latest theories coming out of Harvard. He was from a different time and era. When a handshake and verbal confirmation of *we have a deal* were good as gold. Hicks wanted the personal touch often lost in profit margins and investor satisfaction. I sometimes long for those days in our era of corporate scandal and corruption. But I digress.

This wasn't the first time I'd met Bill Hicks. Last March, when I thought about life after high school, I applied for a job at the Shack. Hicks sat with me to determine my fate.

It didn't matter that I already had position with his company, albeit insignificant and small. Bill met with all personnel even for promotions.

I didn't care. I needed money, and working The Boardwalk would double pay. This would be a definite step up from cheese slinger.

A Texas drawl called out from behind me, "Neil, how goes it partner?"

I dropped my application as my heart raced through my brown tweed sleeves and corduroy pants.

"Hello, Mr. Hicks. How are you today?" I asked scrambling to gather the application.

Hicks looked around as if he was waiting for someone else to show up. "The only Mr. Hicks I know is my father. You can call me Bill, sound good?"

I nodded and handed Bill my application. "I filled out the application and updated my references" I said, pointing at a botThomas portion of the app.

Bill glanced at the application, paused, walked to the wooden railing of the pier, and tossed it over the edge into the ocean. He watched the application float into the Pacific Ocean with a smile. "Don't like paper. It's impersonal. You don't get to know a man by reading paper. Most of it's lies anyway. Let's chat partner, what d'you say?"

I recovered from the sight of my application floating along the waves of the ocean, thinking about the time I took to fill out the damn thing. "That's fine," I said, remembering some of the application's stretched truth. Like my GPA. More of a strong A- student, not straight A's.

Bill wrapped an arm around my neck and steered me toward the Ferris wheel which sat in the center of The Boardwalk. He pointed to the heavens. "You see this here Ferris wheel. It's a marvel of amusement and technology. Our most popular ride. The backbone of TB."

I craned my neck and nodded along impressed by his enthusiasm for the ride. "It's a beauty. I've been on it a time or two."

Bill slapped my side and gave a wide grin. "Good to hear partner. You an Oceanside kid?"

"Born and raised."

Hicks believed The Boardwalk was the most important institution in Oceanside. He wanted people to have fun, escape life, and make him a little money. Financial prosperity was never his motivation. He genuinely believed the theme park could change lives. I didn't know about that. But, if he made money, I had a job and could pay for college and gas. Win for all.

He released his death grip and wandered around the Ferris wheel staring into the sky like he'd never seen it hundreds of times before today. Hicks took off his ten-gallon cowboy hat and placed it over his heart, "God bless America, yahoo."

I watched with interest as he did his ritual around the Ferris wheel and wondered if we'd ever get to an *actual* interview. I enjoyed the cool air and smells of the Pacific. Combination of sea and sand are indescribable.

Hicks placed his hat on his balding head and adjusted it to the right, "You think you can operate this beauty? As you called it..."

"Of course, Mr. Hicks. I've watched your employees operate this beauty from The Shack for months. To get an opportunity would be the highlight of the summer," I said, turning around and pointing at The Shack.

"That's great kid! But, two things. One, don't call me Mr. Hicks, just Bill. That's what people called my father, and he was a dirt bag. Second, I know where The Shack is. Built it and hired you," he said, with a grin.

I gave Hicks a stare and was surprised he remembered our last interview. Thought with his sporadic and playful behavior he didn't pay attention to people and details. He never seemed present. But, he was, always.

Even if Hicks was crazy, he kept people a priority. Hicks even called me when he found out my parents divorced.

"Sorry, Bill. I'll do better."

"You think you can handle the Wheel?"

"Oh, yes, Bill. Be honored to run this ride."

"Good. That's not what I need a worker for. No one starts on the Ferris wheel. Later, son. Later," he said, with a wink.

I scratched my head. Wondered why he led me through the Ferris wheel ritual to tell me no. However, that was Bill, you never know what you'll get. I waited for what would come next in the world of Bill.

Bill stood in the middle of the pier and stared toward a bank of rides, games, and eateries. He held a long look and didn't say a word which seemed to last for five minutes. He moved toward an entrance to a ride, *Dante's Hell.*

DH, as we called it, was a rip-off of *Dante's Inferno* in Coney Island. Hicks didn't seem to mind.

The castle-like structure was painted with a devil holding a pitchfork, werewolves, walls of mirrors, and a casket car that bumped into things on the way through. It was kind of scary, but most people ignored the scary and made out. It was a brilliant way to lure a scared date into a kiss, at least I heard.

"I need someone to run this scary guy. *Dante's Hell*, I thought of the name myself," Hicks said, widening his arms and pointing at a sign with letters written in flames.

I crossed my arms and nodded toward the ride and tried to show excitement, knowing I wanted to work the Ferris wheel. "This is scary," I said.

"You better believe it partner. The scariest ride in California."

I nodded in agreement, then said, "I heard there's one in Coney Island that's scarier."

Hicks glanced over and gave me a stare I would never forget. Like I told him his firstborn was Lucifer himself, "What did you say, boy?"

I retracted my words, to not sound like a moron before I lost the job. "Ugh, well, you know, An idiot friend of mine told me there's a scarier ride at Coney Island called Dante's Inferno. Very similar. He visited it on a family vacation last summer. Dante's Hell is much scarier in my opinion."

Hicks pointed a chubby finger in my chest, "You calling me a cheater? You think I stole the idea for this ride?"

"No way, Bill. I'd never think such a thing."

"Those hacks in Coney Island wouldn't know scary if an armadillo jumped up and bit them in the ass."

Bill became calm and shook his head a couple times and looked back up at me, "I'm messing with you kid. I stole the idea from those Coney Island shit brains. I always say, 'Creativity is the art of copying.'"

The one thing about Hicks was he knew the competition and knew it well. He wanted The Boardwalk to be the best attraction in all the world. Even if you had to copy an East Coast rival. Despite my flippant comment I respected his passion. "You're right. The Boardwalk is leagues ahead of Coney Island or Ocean City. Those guys are minor league and we're the majors."

Hicks paused and gave me a look over, "Holy shit, kid. You know your stuff. Those hacks on the East Coast can't light a kerosene match in a coal mine compared to The Boardwalk."

I never quite understood Hicks analogies and nodded pretending I did, "Hacks."

"Well, we're done here. I'm getting hungry and that means times up. You got the job. Start on Monday, and I'll pay you double what you're making now. Meet in front of DH, 10 AM, and my assistant will show you the ropes."

I gripped Hicks' hand with both of mine and smiled ear to ear. "Thank you so much, sir. You won't be disappointed."

Hicks tipped his hat and smiled. "Call me Bill, and be loyal. You'll do fine."

He backed off and wanted no more of my enthusiastic hand shaking. He disappeared behind a corndog stand.

I gave a fist pump and hoped no one on the pier saw me, glided past the Ferris wheel and gave another look at its massive size. It was a marvel of amusement and technology as Hicks said.

I wandered around the empty pier only being 9:30 AM. No plans and wasn't sure what to do. I wasn't in the mood to talk with my parents about the divorce. If my dad was getting tail on the side, I didn't want to know that either. It sucked all the way around and that was enough for now. I leaned against the wooden railing of the pier and stared out into the endless abyss of the Pacific Ocean.

A hand rested on my shoulder. I turned back expecting to see Hicks or Sherry wanting to make things right. No such luck.

No one there.

I glanced at my shoulder and brushed it off like a Seagull dropped a bomb on me. I scanned left and right not seeing anyone on the empty pier. Only one fisherman at the end. The Boardwalk didn't open for another hour.

I peeked at the Ferris wheel and noticed a car swaying in the morning breeze. I dreamed for a moment of handling the controls I'd watched a hundred times while hanging out with my buddies. I knew I'd start on Dante's Hell, but I'd get to the Wheel. It drew me in.

The base of the Ferris wheel was surrounded by a black iron fence. I walked the perimeter and brushed a hand along the seagull bombed railing, rethinking my actions. I kept an eye on the swaying car not sure why.

A hand swiped against my brown suit sleeve and a cold breeze brushed my face. Not a cold you'd feel in Oceanside in September, much cooler.

I spun around looking for the hand that touched me.

Nothing.

I peeked at the swaying Ferris wheel car and it stopped. Things felt off, and I headed back to the parking lot.

I unlocked and fired up the El Camino and waited a moment to let her old bones warm up. I checked my rearview mirror and noticed a dark haired man walking toward the car.

He tapped on my window and made a sign to roll it down. I obliged and asked if he needed help.

"Be careful kid. The Boardwalk is not a safe place. Ask Sherry."

Before I could say a word, the man walked away and vanished over a sand dune past the parking lot.

EDDIE PEPPITONE's bustled with sounds of Elvis playing from an extra loud jukebox. A waitress wearing a poodle skirt skated by holding a round tray of burgers, Cherry Cokes, and milkshakes. She snapped gum and swayed in time with the music.

Eddie Pep's, as we called it, was just that, a way to pep up your day whether it be birthday, Little League victory, or broken heart, like when Lily Spencer chose Billy Cunduff over me for the eighth grade winter dance. I spent what felt like half a childhood sitting in those squeaky red vinyl booths amused by the sassy waiters and waitresses.

The retro 50's charm faded late in high school when Marilyn Monroe, Elvis, and Fonzie imitators didn't hold the mystique they once did. They were just lame. The in-your-face attitude taking orders saying, "What you want hon? You wanna a milk shake city slicker, or what the hell you want?" It got old.

Despite pleading to eat in a more grown up establishment, Dad brought me to *Pep's* to have our talk. Not sure why to this day. Maybe relive the good ol' days when the family was still happy and not moving toward division. Maybe to cheer him up, or me, or both. I think Dad liked the 50's because it was his formative years. I think in a weird way dad thought his era was superior to the 70's. Most parents think like this. I do.

A metal canister of strawberry milkshake flowed into a ribbed glass. I stirred a wide red straw and could sense an awkward tension in the air above the sounds of "You Ain't Nothin' But a Hound Dog".

Dad spoke through slurps of chocolate shake. "So, you heard?"

"Yep," I said, wiping a glob of shake from the corner of my mouth.

My dad was a good man. He didn't seem like the divorced type. Not sure what that means, but he was as straight-laced as they came. He worked for Texaco as an engineer. Salary, pension, benefits, the entire American Dream package. His employment lasted thirty years for the oil giant, until retirement, the loyal employee every company dreams of. Not what you see today.

Dad flopped open a leather wallet on the table and a black comb fell to the side. He took a pass through his short, slick, dark hair, the hair that fit Pep's, but not the 70's. It explains why he liked the diner after it lost its coolness. Never understood the comb in the wallet.

"Sometimes people fall out of love, kid."

I nodded listening to his Yoda-like wisdom. My brain froze from the shake.

"I know. Mom said the same thing."

Dad reached across the table and salted his fries and added Ketchup, "Love's a funny thing. One minute you're planning life without kids in the house. Trips to Europe.

New hobbies and adventures. The next, you're meeting with lawyers, deciding who's keeping the house."

"Who *will* keep the house?" I asked.

"Lawyer red tape. Won't know anything for a year. Love that house," he said, staring off into the distance. I rewound all the good memories made on 429 Cherry Street.

I listened and realized I knew little about divorce. Do you sign a paper and say, "Good luck?" By the stress on my dad's face it seemed more complex than that.

Gordie Gordon was a byproduct of The Great Depression. His father wasn't a kind man and liked the bottle more than the kids. He didn't believe raising kids involved getting to know them. My dad fought against this mentality like the plague. He was a good dad, involved, and present in our lives. Never missed a game, recital, or big life event.

I took a deep bite into a cheeseburger, wiped my mouth of mayo, and tried to talk through the food. "Is the divorce mutual?"

My dad leaned back against the red vinyl booth and scanned the diner like someone was taping the conversation. Water bubbled up around his brown eyes. He slammed his fist on the table. "Damn, I loved your mom. Still do. I'm so stupid."

I'd never seen my father cry. Maybe once, when his father died of cancer, and they weren't on good terms when it happened. But, this was a rare moment, and I knew the divorce was not mutual.

"Stupid? What do you mean?"

Dad placed a fist against his mouth and gave a hearty burp. I guess he was done crying.

He paused and looked around the diner and made sure no one was listening. He leaned in and spoke with a whisper. "I cheated on your mother."

A red basket of fries were empty. I pushed to the side of the metal table and braced for what I heard. Larry had been right.

"That was stupid. Why'd you do it?"

He slammed his fist on the table again and a French fry popped up in the air. "Don't know what happened... This damn organ has a mind of its own. Faithful to your mother for twenty years. I'm no cheater."

I knew the organ well. It seemed to have a mind of its own. If not, I would've given up on Sherry long ago, and joined a monastery.

"Who was the woman?"

"That's the worst part. She meant nothing. I met her on a business trip."

I waited for Dad to give me more details.

"Flew to Dallas for Texaco's annual conference. I got drunk one night and met a woman in the bar. She was newly divorced. One thing led to another, and we did the deed. Damn that organ. Bastard is strong."

I snorted with bits of burger residue shooting out of my mouth onto the table. "The deed?"

"You know, Hanky Panky..."

"Sex?"

"Yes, son, sex. Hide the salami... submarine races... you don't know the lingo?"

"No, sorry pops. It's not the 50's anymore," I said with a smile.

My dad swirled ice around his glass of Pepsi and sighed with grief. "I told myself, 'One night wouldn't hurt anyone.' She was divorced. The fire in my marriage was on a low burn. She lived on the East Coast, and I, on the West. The-"

"Then... what?"

He rolled his eyes and had a look of embarrassment on

his face. "She called the house and Mom answered. Told her everything."

"Ooh, shit."

"Watch your mouth. The one-night stand was now something problematic. She told Mom I was her soulmate and she couldn't live without me. I won't lie, I was flattered. I sometimes wish I'd heard that from Mom more often. But, can you believe it?"

"I know what it's like to find your soulmate."

"What?"

"Never mind. Did Mom lose her mind?"

My dad nodded and leaned back in the booth and laughed, "I've never seen her so upset. Imagine a volcano exploding and then Texaco dumping all the oil it owns on top. Not pretty."

We both sat back and imagined Mom full of rage and found it funny. My mother freaked out occasionally, like the time our dog pissed on a basket of sandwiches for a picnic. She ran around the park screaming and flailing her arms, like getting stung by a bee. My sister had spit Pepsi through her nose laughing so hard.

"You still like the woman from the East Coast?"

My dad waved off the comment like I said 2+2= 5. "No way. I barely knew her. Your mother is my soulmate and I want to make it work. Though I think it's too late," he said, with a defeated look in his eyes.

"Here's a random question...Why in the hell did you give her our number? That seems like a dumb move for a one-night stand."

"I was drunk. Not thinking straight. Somewhere in my stupid mind I thought giving out the number made it feel more human. I was sick about the entire thing. The guilt unbearable. I'm not good with women. Dated your mother in high school and married her in college. Clueless with anyone, but Mom."

"I know the feeling."

"Lady troubles?"

When I look back on my life, three divorces later, I wonder if the sins of the father are a real thing. My dad was a good man on the outside. Yet, inside, he was bottled up like a shaken soda ready for release. I don't know if the smiles and "everything is fine" persona were real. That affair on the business trip might've been his Woodstock. He had the same insecurities I did. Fear of failure. Trying to make everyone happy. Yet also never looking in the mirror, and wondering why we do what we do.

"I met a girl at The Snack Shack."

He leaned over the table and slapped me on the side of the head. "That a boy. What's her name?"

I hesitated forgetting Sherry wasn't a fake like my prom date. Still, we'd never had an official date, and she kept blowing me off. What is our official title?

"Sherry... Sherry Lewis."

My dad had a mind like a steel trap. Made him a good engineer. He tapped on the table and scratched his head. "Where have I heard that name?" he said, reaching for the Oceanside Gazette sitting on the edge of the table.

"You wouldn't know her. She didn't go to Oceanside High."

"She a friend of Kim's?"

"Come on Dad, I ain't no pedophile. I'd never date a friend of Kim's."

My father held up the paper and pointed at the front news story, "That's it. Is that her?"

A photo of Sherry standing on the steps of the Ocean-side courthouse with head bowed, surrounded by crowds of people, was splashed on the front page. I ripped it out of my dad's hands and skimmed the story mouthing the words, "Holy shit balls."

The story explained Sherry and a couple employees from The Boardwalk were on trial for two deaths at the park. During her shift, while working the Ferris wheel, two young kids were found dead at different areas of the park. One death insinuated that it happened on, or near, the Wheel. It was not clear. No charges were filed for lack of evidence.

"She's a looker," said Dad.

I didn't acknowledge his comment and let the moment settle in for a second. I pieced all the events of the last couple of days together. Sherry's weird response when I invited her for a Ferris wheel ride. Her telling me she worked at The Boardwalk and getting fired. Still not sure why. And the mystery man at my car telling me to be safe.

"I'm cursed like the Chicago Cubs not winning the World Series for ninety years. Except my curse is women. Shit, I meet a beautiful girl and she's a criminal," I said, tossing the newspaper aside on the table.

"Watch your mouth. Technically she wasn't charged with anything. But I'd be careful with this one. That might be tail not worth chasing," my dad said, with a half-smile.

"I've heard 'be safe' in recent memory," I said with a sigh, and stared off in the distance watching a Marilyn Monroe waitress sass a cusThomaser.

Still lame.

Dad and I finished our drinks and drove back home.

My dad was never quite the same after Mom let him go. I understand. Love is a tricky thing.

THE TEMPERATURES ROSE on a warm September day at Sea Lion Beach. Typical crowds of vacationers and out-of-towners thinned as The Boardwalk prepared for fall. Yet because of the warmer weather, business was holding steady.

I sped up the pace from a walk to a slow jog, not wanting to be late for my first day on Dante's Hell. My new supervisor was supposed to show me the ropes. A rendezvous in front of DH at 10 AM. It was 10:03 AM. Dad wouldn't be happy.

The area around DH was absent of people. I glanced at my Star Wars watch, caught my breath, and let out a sigh. No supervisor.

I scanned the pier, walked to the entrance of DH, and peeked inside. A devilish figure with pitchfork, red cape, and evil grin, called out, "Welcome to hell."

A robotic arm swung the pitchfork side to side in time with the voice. I laughed at the lack of scariness and thought about my conversation with Bill Hicks. I hadn't the heart to tell him. Kids were watching *The Texas Chain Saw*

Massacre, Exorcist, and *Jaws.* A robotic talking devil didn't strike fear in the hearts of Oceanside teenagers as Hicks wanted to believe.

No matter. I had a job and was paid to run a ride for people to make out. Not my problem if kids weren't sleeping in their parents beds for the week.

A dark-haired man came from behind the ride and led with a hand outstretched, "Kelvin Rodriguez. Sorry I'm late. Had an issue on the Sea Lion Flyer."

The one ride worth its theme-park-salt was the Flyer. It's an old school wooden roller coaster and had a couple good drops. Sea Lion Flyer was the only roller coaster at TB. Another reason it couldn't compete with bigger parks like Disneyland in Anaheim and Knott's Berry Farm in Buena Park. You need to have bigger rides for all ages.

But it only cost $0.50 compared to $8.95 for Disneyland. Hicks banked on keeping things affordable at TB and hoped to draw different crowds in a tight economy.

I couldn't see the supervisor's face, because he donned a trucker hat pulled down over his eyes. He had a bandana covered in grease hanging from the back of his overalls pocket. Kelvin adjusted the hat on the back part of his head and smiled, "You the new kid? Hicks set me out to train you on DH, correct?"

I nodded and took a second look at his face, the part I could see. My heart sank. I knew this guy. He was Sherry's ex-boyfriend. I gave a half smile, still staring at his face hoping to make a match and ensure not to make an ass out of myself if I was wrong.

"Well kid, a monkey could run this ride. Not saying you are one, but if you can push a couple buttons and pull a few levers you'll be scaring the shit out of people in no time."

I held back a laugh, from the "scaring" part.

Then it clicked. I didn't know what Sherry's ex looked like. Knew he worked at the park. No, this guy was the mystery man who told me to be careful in the parking lot. I waved my arms like a crazy clown trying to get a laugh. "Hello, you don't remember me?" I said, framing my face with my hands.

Kelvin stared down at a clipboard, scribbled a note, and glanced back at me. He raised an eyebrow from the clown dance. "Excuse me. I've never seen you in my life. Hicks sent me to train a new guy. That's you. Sorry, bro. I'd know if we met. I don't forget faces."

I looked for a Candid Camera crew to tell me this was a prank. I couldn't believe this guy. I either was losing my mind, which is possible, or he was lying. I just saw him in the parking lot, and I too don't forget faces.

"So... You don't recall tapping on the window of an awesome '69 El Camino, pristine, telling me to be safe?" I said.

Kelvin gave an almost smile, liking the car comment, lowered the clipboard and switched to a deep stare that wasn't pleasant. He clipped a pen to the top and tapped on my chest. "Listen dickhead, I don't know you. Don't care to know you. I'm here to train you, and that's it. You ready or not? Stop the chit chat and let's get to it."

I put up my hands in surrender and still thought he was crazy for not knowing me. "Sorry, yes. Let's get after it."

Kelvin's face washed back to a pleasant smile and acted like he didn't just call me a dickhead.

"Good. Dante's Hell is a favorite on The Boardwalk, the scariest ride in California. Mr. Hicks wants all employees to give every rider a great experience. Attitude is everything," Kelvin said, turning his back, and admiring the rest of the park on the pier. Only a handful of people were on the pier, mostly fishermen.

I nodded and tried to have a better attitude. Bill Hicks was the most passionate dude for theme parks in all the land, at least our corner of the world. I didn't know if I shared that passion. But, he was paying me well, and I would be anything he wanted me to be.

I clapped my hands together. "Yep. I'll ride the shit out of Dante's Hell."

Kelvin stared at me and wrote something on his clipboard. I realized the response made little sense and sounded sexual.

"Ugh, I mean... anyone riding Dante's Hell will be scared out of their minds. That's a promise," I said, lifting a finger. Again I realized I looked ridiculous and didn't know what passion for TB entailed.

Kelvin rolled his eyes and pointed to DH, painted with a bloody lettered sign, "Why don't you calm down? Let's take a look at this baby and get a feel for the controls. Feel her out."

That sounded sexual.

We stood behind what looked like a wooden pulpit in church, where the preacher would yell and explain why rock and roll was ruining America. That's at least how I imagined it.

The top of the pulpit had round silver knobs with blinking green and red lights, multiple switches, and a microphone like in a drive thru burger joint.

"Whoa, that's a lot of buttons," I said.

"No fear. Most of them don't concern you. These are the ones you need to worry about," Kelvin said, brushing over a bank of flashing red and green buttons.

I acted interested and pressed a button to see what

would happen. A car shaped liked a black casket rushed from a left dark tunnel and lurched to a stop in front of the pulpit. The casket adorned with red and yellow flames and "Dante's Hell" tattooed on the front half.

"What the hell you doing rookie? You'll get someone hurt."

I apologized and a weird sensation came over me. I was getting passionate about rides. When the casket pulled up, it was a rush of lighting. I was in control. My life that summer felt out of control. Maybe giving a bunch of horny teenagers a few minutes of fun was something. Something I could get passionate about, at least for a summer.

Kelvin wrote something on the clipboard which I assumed was me failing the training, and I'd be crawling back to The Snack Shack any minute.

"Good... well, you didn't totally screw up. That button brings the cars to the loading dock. A DH worker will load the passengers in at that point. You need to worry about these..." Kelvin said, pointing to another bank of lights and levers.

I fondled my chin, and sighed, pretended to think the running of DH wasn't monkey-work. Kelvin took his job seriously, maybe too seriously, but I admired the effort. After a thirty-minute training, this monkey was ready to scare the teenagers of Oceanside. Or not. At least give them a few minutes to make out.

Kelvin wrote a couple more notes on his clipboard, which I was certain was overkill, and attempted to look professional. He thanked me for the time and explained Boardwalk policies. After navigating scheduling, how to use a sick day, and pay, Kelvin reached under the wooden pulpit. "Welcome aboard," he said, smiling and handing me a TB official uniform.

The shirt was blue with two buttons and a small sliver of yellow across the neck. It had matching pants which were blue, a little tight. A logo of The Boardwalk plastered on a right pocket with a silhouette of the Ferris wheel in the background.

Kelvin fiddled around in his pocket and pulled out a silver name tag with my name on it. "Now it's official."

I smiled and felt peace about it all. This wasn't the dream job. But, it was a job, and now I had money to pay for college and gas. It was better than minimum wage at the Shack.

"See ya 9 AM Thomasorrow. Don't be late or Mr. Hicks will lose his mind."

I nodded, Kelvin fiddled with a couple knobs on DH, and left the pier.

I still wanted to know why Kelvin didn't recognize me. Maybe it wasn't him? For another time. I started work in the morning.

Even if a monkey could do it.

I WANTED TO RUN. The constant fighting between my parents and Kim being the golden child of the family and my voice never heard. I thought leaving home after high school was a rite of passage. My parents went off to college, married after graduation. Why not me?

With no off campus college experience at Oceanside Community College, at least I could rent an apartment and create a dorm-like atmosphere. If it was cheap.

"Is that water dripping from the light," I asked, flipping a switch on and off, and scanning the rundown apartment.

The landlord wiped dust from a window sill and didn't notice me staring him down. No amount of dusting could erase the smell. I didn't know what landlords were supposed to look like. But, wearing sweatpants and a stained wife beater tank top didn't shout professionalism.

"Come on, boys. I'm only asking $400 a month. Beach views. All utilities paid. You can't find an apartment in Sea Lion Beach for *this* price," he said, scratching his crotch and flicking a cockroach from the kitchen counter.

Larry found a job in LA doing menial tasks for a movie

production company. Working craft services and running errands for B-movie actors. A start into the movie-biz.

He didn't want to live with his parents either. Larry believed college education was optional for aspiring famous directors. Stanley Kubrick was a photographer and never went to film school. Larry worshipped the filmmaker and saw no need for higher education, which didn't matter either way because inheritance from a dead uncle gave him time.

The "Roach Motel," as we called it, was a stone's throw from The Boardwalk and Larry didn't mind the thirty-minute drive to LA. We'd be away from our parents and still close enough to drop by when needing laundry done.

"Beach views, yes. Cheap rent, yes, can't argue there. But, when was the last time this place was cleaned? Was Richard Nixon president?"

I didn't mind a little dirt or yellow shag carpet with stains, like the driveway after I change the El Camino's oil. But the roaches were driving dune buggies amidst the dust.

The landlord rolled his eyes and examined our applications. He appeared to be picking something green out of his teeth. "It's only $400, guys. Don't get picky."

I rolled my eyes knowing the money I'd spend to buy flea killer and roach spray. My dad taught me to budget with three principles: pay your savings, pay your bills, and pay someone in need. The money from TB would be a raise. However, things were tight when trying to save, pay bills, and help others. Added rent wouldn't help my cause.

Larry burst into the living room and framed it with his hands. He didn't care for the apartment but we were on our own and could walk to the beach. That's all that mattered to him, and me. And having space to watch movies and learn the craft of editing film without parents admonishing Larry to get a real job, like an engineer, made the Roach Motel heaven.

"The projector can go here. TV over there. What you think, Neil?"

I nodded and pretended to care, still thinking about the landlord picking his teeth. I wouldn't be fussy. It was Larry's place. He knew I needed money for college and gas. Money for Larry was never an issue with the inheritance. He only charged $50 for my share. I needed a bookshelf for my favorite novels and a space to play records. That's it.

I was running, not wanting to deal with reality. The Eddie Peppitone's conversation with Dad made me lose respect. He was a good guy, but cheating on Mom was heavy and wrong. I don't think teenagers can understand much. I didn't have a category for cheating fathers. But, looking back now, I'd probably be more gracious.

My parents still lived under the same roof. They pretended everything was okay around Kim and I. We heard the fights late at night. It was usually Dad pleading for forgiveness, and Mom saying, "Do you love that whore?"

I wanted out, and the Roach Motel would have to do, for now.

I wiped down a greasy window with the sleeve of my sweatshirt. When it cleared the panorama of the Pacific Ocean came into view. A shade to the right you could see the Ferris wheel. A vulture perched on the highest peak of the Wheel staring out toward the ocean. I smirked, thinking about Bill Hicks' love affair with the ride. Not sure why he loved it so. But, to be honest, I was drawn to it too.

Larry bumped me out of the way trying to get a peek through the dirty window. His eyes widened, and he elbowed me in the side. "You see that?"

"The Ferris wheel? She's a beauty, isn't she?"

"Boobies. Big boobies!"

"What?" I asked, cupping my hands around my face trying to deflect the sunlight coming inside the dingy apartment.

"Check 'em out. Those are beautiful."

There was a large chested woman roller skating across The Boardwalk. Her shorts seemed to be missing fabric. She was oblivious to Larry drooling on the window because of her headphones plugged into a Sony Walkman.

"Are boobs all you think about?" I asked, more focused on the vulture at the moment.

"Yes... well... yes. You don't?"

"No. I have other important things to occupy my mind. Like a new job starting in an hour. Fleetwood Mac in a couple days. Sherry. That vulture."

"Sherry? The bimbo who ghosted you at the movies? You're telling me you never think about touching her round mounds of fun?"

I punched Larry in the side of the head "First, she's not a bimbo. Second, round mounds of fun, really? Besides, we're just taking things slow."

"Slow? So slow, I never see her."

"We made headway the other day, at the beach. She opened up. It was like a deep conversation."

"I'm sure it was great..." Larry said, obviously not hearing a word and staring. "Damn, look at those things jiggle."

"Are you even listening?"

"Huh? What? Not really."

I opened the back door of the apartment and let Larry finish his stare-a-thon. I stood on a small balcony facing the pier, getting a better look at the vulture. I called to Larry, "If you're done staring at that helpless woman. Come see the vulture. I've never seen anything like it on Sea Lion Beach. Lots of seagulls... never vultures. You?"

Larry shook the fog from a boob-watching haze and came back to earth. "Vulture? What are you a bird watcher now? Never seen one on Sea Lion Beach before."

"That sounds like something somebody just said. Look at how he's perched on top of the Ferris wheel. It's like something is dead underneath and he's waiting to swoop down and gobble its remains."

"Maybe a dead seagull is below. Like the time we fed one a corndog."

"Kind of creepy."

"Who cares? Can we decide on the apartment so you can get to work, and so we don't hold this lovely gentleman up any longer?"

The sweaty landlord came out onto the balcony and picked his sweatpants out from his butt crack. "You fellas need to decide. I have interested clients who will snatch this place up."

I peeked at Larry and he glanced back at me. We gave each other the thumbs up.

That morning we signed the papers and paid first and last rent. And a cleaning deposit, which was a joke considering the smells that never left our apartment for the entire summer.

After work that evening, we both moved in all our earthly possessions. Not much. The Roach Motel was disgusting, but it was ours, and that's all that mattered.

I reclined in a chair on the patio and wondered if the vulture ever got that seagull.

WE STOOD in a circle between the Ferris wheel, Dante's Hell, and a bank of other games. One Ball designed to rip off children and deny them... the largest stuffed bear on the planet behind the group of Boardwalk employees.

I placed my hands in my pockets and scanned the circle looking at fellow TB workers I'd spend the fall with. There were a couple people chatting who knew one another probably from slinging corndogs at Captain Dog or manning vomit inducing rides like The Spinner.

Kelvin still pretended to not remember me, and after training, seemed standoffish. I didn't know what to think.

Bill Hicks expected to make an appearance and give the famous, or infamous depending how you see it, Boardwalk Way speech. He wanted to ensure all employees knew their mission. Fun, inspiration, and service, if I remember correctly.

As we waited, I stared up at the Ferris wheel and thought about the vulture a few hours earlier. I glanced at the ground and looked for a dead seagull choking on a corndog. The vulture was nowhere to be found and no dead children or seagulls were in view. The Wheel squeaked in the wind sitting empty as the park was not open to the public yet.

I heard the rustling of feet and saw the group of twelve standing at attention like an army platoon waiting for orders. I joined the crowd and watched Bill Hicks bustle his way to the center of the circle. He was wearing typical three-piece grey suit, a little dated for the times, and no cowboy hat. Instead, he wore a Native Indian headdress. Odd. Full of feathers and exploding with red, blue, and yellow vertical painted lines around the base.

I smiled and scanned the circle not believing what I was seeing. *Was this an act?* The rest of the crew didn't find the humor. They were locked in on Hicks and held onto every word.

"Howdy, friends. Most of you know who I am. But, for the uninitiated and new employees, I welcome you to The Boardwalk family. My name is Bill Hicks. You can call me Bill. Never Mr. Hicks, that's my father, and he's dead. We are building a world class theme park at Sea Lion Beach that will rival the Coney Islands, Ocean Cities, and maybe one day, the Disneylands of the world. Yee Haw."

I smirked and knew Hicks was a little crazy, maybe a lot. Disneyland made TB look like a badly run seven-year-old birthday party, without the pony. And TB was nowhere near the quality and draw of Coney Island, so I'm told.

The crowd nodded and locked into Hick's words like the State of the Union Address from Jimmy Carter. He was kooky but kind of inspiring in a weird old man from Texas kind of way.

I wanted to ask about the headdress but most of the employees didn't seem to care, except one, Chet Wilson. He caught my attention and pointed at Hicks head, shrugged, and mouthed the words, "What?"

Chet became a quick friend. He too was in the throes of leaving high school and entering the abyss of the college years. He was in his second year of offseason work at TB and was trying to pay for college. He had a good sense of humor, like Larry, but less perverted.

Oblivious of Hicks turning in his direction. I tried to warn Chet with my eyes.

Hicks gave Chet a stare like he knew he was being mocked but would give him a second chance. He kept on with his speech, "You may wonder why this Texan is wearing a Native America headdress? The Sioux tribe have a special place in my heart. They hail from the Dakotas. A mighty tribe, loyal tribe, and these feathers are authentically worn by their Chiefs. I want the employees of The Boardwalk to be loyal, hard-working, and enduring. Like our Indian friends."

Bill was a visual teacher. You never knew what kind of prop or gimmick he'd use to teach a life lesson or apply to cusThomaser service. He reminded me of the way Jesus taught parables in the Bible. If I recall, the disciples were always confused. No different with Hicks. His allusions still baffle me today.

"The Boardwalk Way is one of fun, inspiration, and service. You'll be loyal to each other, and the cusThomaser. Like our Sioux friends," Hicks said, adjusting the headdress as it slumped to the side.

Chet pretended to yawn.

"We invite the busy people of California, and visitors from around the world, to an opportunity of escape. An escape from the stress of jobs, family, failing economy, and life. Not just escape, but escape to reenter a world of fun. A world where teenagers' hearts race, scared to death on Dante's Hell. Mothers, fathers, brothers, and sisters screaming out their lungs as they drop on Sea Lion Flyer. The look in a child's eye when they knock over the milk jugs on One Ball. Awe and wonder when crowds watch one of our shows on American history."

I crossed my arms and knew One Ball was a scam. In a million attempts with friends we never knocked over those damn jugs. We heard they were weighted with sand and lead. I'd later find out it was true.

I peeked up at the Ferris wheel and remembered the day when I felt a presence like someone touching me. Wished that someone was Sherry.

Hicks droned on and my attention span waned. I wanted to work. I shook it off and tried to endure the rest of the speech.

"Inspiration. The second value is inspiration at The Boardwalk. We perspire to inspire. We want kids to look at the design of this...," Hick said, pointing at The Ferris wheel, "... and say, I could build something beautiful and massive and a technological wonder like the Wheel. When we put on shows about American history, we want people to consider this great country and the difference we can make for her progress. I'm an American and without the freedoms here I'd be nothing. Yee Haw."

The shows were the worst. You'll hear more about that later. But, dressing up in an Abraham Lincoln costume and giving the Gettysburg Address was not my idea of fun.

Despite the kookiness of Hicks, he expressed fresh ways for understanding themes parks I never considered. He believed people were not only coming to have fun, but to be changed, and think. I didn't go to TB to think. I wanted to meet girls. But Hicks was an outside-the-box thinker. Maybe I needed to take TB more serious.

"Service. Built my empire on service. Never liked the typical business theories of Harvard and botThomas line thinking. I believe if you treat people well, you treat them like family, they'll be loyal. Or, like my Lord and Savior, it's more blessed to give than receive. People first, give first. When people are served and treated well, they'll come back and spend money," Hicks said, with a chuckle. "Jesus doesn't want us broke, does he?" and went back to his speech.

"I joke, friends. Making money is not a bad thing. But it's not what gets this old Texan out of bed each day. I want to serve you and the people of TB. Service is King, botThomas line is Queen. Who doesn't like the old lady to rub your toes once in a while?"

The group looked at one another and didn't know what his weird analogy meant. Typical Hicks, but people were loyal, like the Sioux. He was eccentric, but you couldn't help but love the guy.

Bill finished the speech and the twelve of us clapped and shouted. I never knew working for a quasi-theme park would be so serious. Bill wanted to be the best and wow the cusThomaser, whether they were riding the Flyer or getting ripped off at One Ball. I adhered to the Boardwalk Way most of the time. Yet, working with the public is never glamorous. People are people, and it' hard to serve when people bitch and moan. The cusThomaser is not always right.

Hicks bowed, raised his headdress, and spent the next five minutes shaking hands with all the employees, and welcoming them to the family. That's the guy he was. He was crazy but meant well.

I found myself off to the side alone not knowing many

people. Chet came up shaking his head and picking at his tooth, "You believe that guy? Fun, inspiration, service, huh?"

"It wasn't that bad. I'm kind of inspired for work Thomasorrow."

"Please tell me you don't buy into all the BS? I came here to make money and pay for college. I'll wear a monkey suit if I get a check. The values of TB are not my primary concern, right?"

I smiled at Chet and knew what he was talking about. I didn't care all that much about the values of TB and knew this wasn't a thirty-year career. Hoped by the same time next year I'd get a job editing the school paper, or writing articles about firemen rescuing cats from trees in the Ocean-side Gazette. Something to get the writing career on the map. I'd put up with Hicks' craziness for a while if it helped me get a writing job. That meant needing to stay in school.

Chet held out a hand, "I'm Chet Wilson. Hope I didn't get you in trouble with my laughing. It's my second season here at TB and heard the Boardwalk Way before. Hope I don't come off jaded. I'm not. There are worse jobs, like fast food."

I nodded and could relate with fast food jobs. I don't think slinging cheese sauce at The Snack Shack was much different.

"No worries, Hicks' speech got long."

"Don't buy into the service crap. This place is not about service, it's about money. Don't let Hicks tell you otherwise."

I scratched my head, "Really?"

"Wait until we have a budget meeting."

"Budgets? I work rides. Why do I care about the budget?"

"That's what I thought. But Hicks wants everyone to know where we are, financially. If we are struggling, workers get the blame because our service is not up to par. Be ready. Last season we sucked balls when it got freezing in December. Somehow we got blamed for an act of God."

I scratched my head and still thought Hicks was a good guy from what I could tell. He treated me well, like family, and I couldn't blame him for wanting to make money. I knew his obsession with beating the guys at Coney Island and being the best theme park in the land was unhealthy. We all have our obsessions, like Sherry Lewis.

"What ride you working?" I asked Chet.

"Ferris wheel."

"Ooh, I'd love to work that one. I'm on Dante's Hell."

"I did DH last summer. Not so scary, more make-out central."

I laughed knowing it was true despite not having any experience, with the making out part that is. "How do you get on The Wheel?"

"Kind of random. The supervisor shifts us around depending on what staff is available. You'll get a shot. But to be honest, I don't like it."

"Why not?"

"Every time I work the ride my sThomasach hurts."

"You happen to eat a chili dog at Rathan's? Trust me, stay away."

"No, it's not that. I've ridden the diarrhea train after Rathan's. There's like a weird presence, like someone watches you, when you're near the Wheel. Can't explain it."

"Like someone touching you?"

"Yeah... but not in a girlfriend good way. It feels heavy and real, but no one is ever there."

"I know what you're talking about. It's probably nothing. Maybe we can talk to Bill Hicks if it becomes a problem," I said, glancing at The Wheel sitting quietly.

Chet paused, thought about his next words, and stared at the wooden pier floor, "You hear about the dead kids?"

"I think so. Last summer?"

"Yeah. There's a girl and a couple employees who went to trial. It's done now. A black mark on The Boardwalk. But honestly, it hasn't stopped business. People are fascinated with things that appear haunted. At least that's the rumor."

"Haunted?"

"No one knows, maybe it's in our heads. Still, ever since those kids died people think The Boardwalk is haunted. Weird things been happening since that day, like..."

"Like what?"

"You know, the Ferris wheel and other things. Hard to explain. Like when a faucet shot water in the air when no one was using it. Rides turning on with no help. Weird stuff."

I didn't want Chet to know I knew Sherry yet, "Did you know any of the employees were on trial?"

"Not well. There was a hot chick, Sherry Lewis, who took it hard. She quit, and rumor is she spent time in the loony bin."

"She went crazy?"

"No one knows for sure. But she's still around."

"I know... I mean, oh."

"Shit happens. Part of living in this messed up world. I'm just glad we have rock and roll."

"Huh?"

"When stuff in life sucks, I'm glad I can just relax and spin my Fleetwood Mac records."

"You a fan?" I asked.

"Number One fan."

"You can't be Number One... if I hold the spot. I'm obsessed. You free Thomasorrow night?"

"Why?"

"I got tickets to Fleetwood Mac at The Greek Theater. My friend Larry can't go, and I'd love to not go alone. Kind of embarrassing going to a concert solo."

Chet lit up a Camel unfiltered and smiled, "I'm in! We'll see who the bigger fan is..."

I knew then that Chet and I would be good friends.

LARRY'S FEET draped over the end of the gold couch that itched bare skin, a thrift store deal for those on a tight budget. It matched the yellow shag carpet of the Roach Motel.

He flipped through *Film Review* magazine complaining about the latest James Bond film *Moonraker* starring Roger Moore. The review didn't align with Larry's particular cinematic tastes.

"It's a shame Sean Connery is no longer Bond. Roger Moore's a hack," said Larry, sitting up to acknowledge my existence in the small apartment.

"I like Moore. Why's he a hack?" I asked.

Larry stood to his feet wearing a velour bathrobe looking like a wannabe film star strung out on drugs, minus the stardom, and Larry didn't do drugs, "Oh, no. Please tell me uniformed filmgoer you're not comparing these two blokes. Connery versus Moore is like comparing the acting ability of Robert De Niro and Ron Howard from *Happy Days*. Not even in the same stratosphere."

"Who gives a shit? 007 is supposed to be a fun action

movie. Obvious plot. You get a good-looking guy, throw in a beautiful love interest, a crime to solve, and a couple car chases. You don't need Marlon Brando."

Larry blushed, and I thought he would blow a blood vessel in his forehead. He threw the paper on the couch, "I'll let this one go. We've made so much progress in your film education. It's good you're going to Fleetwood Mac, or I'd tell you what I really think about Roger Moore. You find someone to go with?"

As Larry asked the question someone banged on the front door. Our first guest to the new place. It was Chet.

I unlocked the door. "Your ears must've been burning," I said, giving Chet a hand slap.

He smiled and waved at Larry who was adjusting the belt on his robe.

"Chet will join me for Fleetwood Mac because of his fine music tastes. Unlike some people I know," I said, punching Larry in the arm.

"Movie scores are good music."

Chet gave me a look over, "Good to see I didn't overdress. I wasn't sure what to wear. Great minds think alike, I guess," Chet said, noticing we both were wearing the same t-shirt of a Fleetwood Mac *Rumors* album cover.

Larry grabbed his forehead like caressing a migraine, "You guys look ridiculous. No one wears band t-shirts to see the actual band. That's bush league. You'll look like dick holes."

I said, "Sorry about my friend. He prizes himself on fashion, as you can tell by the stained velour bathrobe he's wearing," I said with a smile.

I went to the back bedroom and came back with a different shirt on. It was a *Star Wars* t-shirt with Luke Skywalker posing a light saber and Leia around his leg.

"Much better," Larry said, rolling his eyes.

"Chet and I heading out so we don't get stuck in traffic."

Larry waved, disappeared to his bedroom, and we headed our separate ways.

I fired up the El Camino and made small talk with Chet realizing we didn't know each other well. It kind of felt like an awkward first date. Once I'd hoped Sherry would be in the passenger seat, but this would do for now. It was a needed escape from the new job, parents' divorce, and the revelations of my possible criminal love interest.

I'd saved all my Snack Shack money for three months to get tickets. I couldn't wait to see Lindsey Buckingham shred on guitar, hear the angelic singing of Stevie Nicks, and hear my favorite song, "Go On Your Way." It seemed to be another theme for the summer.

Chet leaned over to the eight-track playing "Rumors" and turned the volume down. He had a look of concern on his face. He paused a couple beats and thought through his words, "Neil, I know we barely know each other, but I need to tell you something."

"What's up, man? If it's about Larry, I'm sorry. He's like a fine wine. Gets better with age and time. He'll grow on you.'"

"No. Larry's great. I need to talk to you about The Boardwalk."

I could see the concern in his eyes and didn't know where the conversation was headed. "Okay... Am I sucking at my job? It's only been a couple days. I can do better. Did Rodriguez say something?"

Chet shoot it off, and looked away from me and out the passenger window saying, "There's shit going down at TB that's not good. Like terrible shit."

"Damn. I left the power on Dante's Hell before leaving the other night, didn't I?"

Chet chuckled dryly, "No. Much worse."

I waited.

"Remember when I told you a couple kids died last summer. Well, the bad shit's related to the trial."

"I'd think so. When people die, it's never good for business."

Chet didn't find the attempt at humor amusing and went back to the issue at hand. "Rumor is, there's a big cover up going down. People got paid off to keep quiet. You ever wonder why the park is still open and people keep coming? Business as usual. Most parks would've never recovered from the lawsuits and insurance hikes. You're right, dead kids are never good for business. I think Bill Hicks is behind it."

I watched the trees and cars race by on Highway 101 in the setting California sun. I let Chet's words settle for a moment. I wasn't sure how Sherry's story jived with it all.

"Do you know for sure? Who told you?"

"I can't know 100 percent. My source is reliable, though, and used to work at the park. She has no reason to lie."

"I guess I'm confused. I saw the newspaper article about the trial and the employees involved. People must know what happened, right? Wouldn't that scare people away from the park?"

"You'd think, but the trial thrown out. They said 'not enough conclusive evidence' for a conviction. The park, Bill Hicks, and employees, weren't charged with any crime. The problem is, I was there, and so were others. We saw with the dead kids with our own eyes. I don't know how the trial is thrown out unless someone was paid off. It was like it never happened. And, I don't know why the parents didn't file a civil suit and sue the pants off TB, knowing their kids died on our watch. I would've," Chet said, wiping a tear from his cheek.

We arrived in the parking lot of the Greek Theater, the outdoor concert venue in Griffith Park. We sat and watched mobs of people herding into the concert. It felt like Chet and I were having a break-up conversation, and we just started dating. Awkward.

We continued the conversation making our way to the front entrance of the Greek.

"It makes sense, I guess. So, what are you saying? What does this mean? What do we do?"

"I don't want you caught up in a shit storm. We're just kids, have our entire lives ahead of us, and not supposed to be involved in this kind of stuff. TB is a seasonal job and not a dream career. At least not for me. But, I think we need to be careful. I wanted you to know," Chet said, as we handed our tickets to the attendants.

We scanned the concessions to find something to drink.

Chet was a fun and good-hearted kid. I thanked him for being honest with me even before he knew me. The summer of '79 was a crazy time and would only get crazier knowing what we now knew.

"You think Bill Hicks is a bad guy? I get such mixed signals on the Texan."

Chet paused and reached for a wallet to pay for a soda at the snack bar, "I don't know. He seems like a genuine guy, and then I hear he's paying people off, and I don't know what to think. Maybe be careful of the Texan, good ole boy routine. It might be akin to the shows at Starlight Theater, just a show."

Hicks became a father figure when my parents

divorced. Granted, a weird and sporadic one. I needed someone older to talk to, and he became my metaphorical crying shoulder. He always made time if I asked. I never got the vibe he was shady, but people are people. I don't want to believe Bill ever did anything illegal.

I paid for my soda and took a sip, trying to embrace all the new revelations. "Why you still working at TB knowing what you know?" I asked.

"Eight bucks an hour. Everyone has their price, right?"

I smiled, because it was true. An eighteen-year-old searching for a better paying job in Oceanside with no experience and only The Snack Shack on the resume, no chance. I never pretended to be a saint. I'm not saying I'd do anything for a buck, but that summer, I might've sold my body in the streets if anyone would pay. Maybe I wanted to live in denial of something being off at TB. Everyone has their price, right?

"Do other people know about the possible payoffs? Stuff going down..."

"I don't know, except maybe you, me, and my source."

"Can you tell me more about the source? Or is it classified, James Bond?" I said with a grin.

"I sure can. She's standing right there," Chet said, aiming his soda straw and waving at a red haired girl walking toward us.

It was Sherry Lewis.

Soda almost shot through my nose as I tried to compose myself at the sheer beauty of Sherry in her painted on bellbotThomas jeans, and confusion of why the hell Sherry was at the concert... and was Chet's source.

Sherry sipped on a red, soda straw and gave me blinky eyes. She had me in her tractor beam. Whatever reason she and Chet gave for being at the concert seemed insignificant at the moment. I wanted to soak her in for a second.

"Hi, Neil. How've you been?"

I took a deep breath and tried to not sound like a moron.

"Uh, good... No. Make it great. I'm great! You heard? I got a job at The Boardwalk. You're looking at the new ride runner for Dante's Hell. Getting ready for college, you know, living the dream. Oh, and I got my own place now. So, great."

She smiled and swayed to the side, and I could tell wanted to say something more. "That's great, Neil. Thrilled for you. A lot has happened for me in the last couple of weeks. So yeah, I didn't call you back. Kind of dropped the ball on that one," she said, not wanting to stare in my direction.

I waved her off and pretended I didn't even know she broke my heart and ghosted me again. But again, I didn't care all that much. The bellbottoms were clouding rational thought at this point.

"No problem. You're busy. I'm busy too with the job, college, concert, apartment upkeep. You know, lots of stuff," I said.

"Not true. I'm not that busy. Just going through some stuff. It's hard finding a job with your face plastered on the front page of the paper as potential criminal," she said her eyes puffing up with redness.

I pretended to not of see the article and asked her to explain, "Did you get voted Ms. Oceanside?"

Sherry slugged me in the arm, "No, stupid. Involved in a court case and it made front page news. Which is not saying much in this town."

"I'm sure it was no big deal. What brings you here tonight? You know Chet?"

"I don't know how much you heard. Chet invited me tonight. He was scheming behind the scenes."

I glanced at Chet and gave a raised eyebrow, "What's going on, Harr-?"

"Chet's a big Fleetwood Mac fan and already had a ticket. When he met you, I guess he recognized your name from a previous conversation we had."

"She's my source. And, I might've heard you have a thing for her."

"She told you?" I said, hiding my face in the soda cup. I found it hard to imagine I made so much of an impression with our previous encounters. I marveled at the plan that was unfolding in front of my eyes and appreciated Harry's willingness to play cupid, in my dateless existence, and try to bring Sherry and I together. I wanted to be mad for being lied to, but I couldn't. Sherry was near me, at a Fleetwood Mac concert. That was good enough.

I smiled at Sherry with hesitation, still never knowing where the hell we stood. "So, Hicks's a bad guy?"

"Think so. I can't say for certain, but everything points that way. We want you to be safe, and TB is not what you think it is. It's got issues."

I nodded.

"What now?"

"Will you go on a date with me to the Fleetwood Mac concert?" Sherry asked.

I paused, looked at Chet, and back at Sherry. "I guess. If you're into ride monkeys who work at theme parks?"

"I am tonight," Sherry said. She took my arm and we made our way to the seats.

Our first and only real date of the summer.

SHE SWAYED in my arms to the sounds of "Go On Your Way" and "Landslide." I took a deep inhale of her smell. A potpourri of coconut and freshly mowed meadow. Was it her perfume or hair? I didn't know and didn't care. I finally had the treasure of summer love. The girl of my dreams. Sherry Lewis.

Fleetwood Mac played an encore set and disappeared behind black curtains of the Greek Theater. We followed the herd of people to the car and spent a few minutes making out before heading home. It was a night forever etched in my mind. The weirdness and pain of the summer of '79 seemed small. It couldn't be any more perfect, at least for the moment.

Only one problem.

Most of it was a dream.

I awoke in the Roach Motel apartment yelling out for help and sporting an erection. Not only did I not make out with Sherry that night, the dream turned into a nightmare that haunts me today.

The night of Fleetwood Mac and a date with Sherry

always mingled with Bill Hicks. Not sure what my therapist thinks about the connection.

Hicks was holding my neck against the wall to entrance of Dante's Hell. He was spitting and yelling venomous threats about DH being the scariest damn ride in the world. I explained how I wanted to make it scarier, and he didn't like my excuses. I didn't know what to do.

It was like when you're running and your feet are in quicksand. You can't seem to outrun the rabid dog, shark, or scary beast of choice. When I had the dream, it always felt heavy. Like real, too real. I couldn't escape the grip of Hicks no matter what.

Half a dozen nights during the summer, the dream visited. Never had the Sherry one again. One can wish. However, I daydreamed about it more times than I can count.

Despite not swapping spit at the concert, it was a fruitful foray into the world of Sherry. I learned about her childhood and absent father. He bailed when she was five, went for cigarettes and never came home. Sherry remembered the day. Her mother worked hard at a waitress job and trying to raise two kids on a low wage and tips.

Sherry found a job at TB when things got hard for the family. She felt obligated as the oldest sibling to do her part. When Sherry got fired for the deaths of the kids, she was destroyed. Sick over the kids, but she also wanted to help the family and couldn't. They lost their apartment and couch surfed between family and friends for months.

She didn't share all the details of what happened at TB when the kids died, but she made clear it was not her fault and she still didn't know what happened that night. Sherry felt set up and wasn't sure why she was thrown under the bus. I believed her. I'd believe anything she said. There was an authenticity in her eyes when she spoke under the marijuana haze of the Greek Theater.

I rolled out of bed and limped to the kitchen table, shaking off cobwebs of sleep and nightmares. Larry played with an eight millimeter role of film on the table and gave me a grin, "You enjoy the concert loser? I heard it was awesome."

I slapped Larry some skin and rubbed a tired hand through a messy mop of hair, "Dude, you're the best friend of the year. Giving up your ticket meant I could meet up with Sherry. Plus, Fleetwood Mac was on their game last night."

"Glad it worked out. I know your love cup was empty. Hope refilled. So...?"

I shook my head *no* and tried to come up with a convincing reason for not scoring with Sherry, "It was great. Fleetwood Mac played for two hours. Best concert of my life."

"No, Neil. Sherry. First, second, third... need to know. I gave up my ticket, did you give up your pants?"

"You're a pervert. Our relationship is not just about physical touch. It's deeper. We talked about hopes, dreams, and childhood struggles."

"Boooring. All relationships with girls are about touch. Did you get tongue?"

I punched Larry in the arm, flipped open a cupboard, and poured a bowl of Frosted Flakes and milk. "Sherry's not a toy to meet my sexual needs. She has feelings, ya know? You wouldn't understand."

"There's the answer. Any dude talking about feelings struck out swinging," Larry said, taping a piece of film roll together and examining it closely like a scientist looking into a microscope.

I plopped down with my cereal and watched Larry work on his reel of film. "You ever have dreams?" I asked.

"Like goals, aspirations?"

"No, nighttime dreams."

"Every night. Holding an Oscar for Best Director. The big booby lady we saw on the beach the other day. And, saving a kitten from a burning building. Kind of weird. You?"

"Yeah, normal stuff. But lately, I've been having ones about Bill Hicks."

"Is he naked?"

"No, dick hole. It's quite terrifying. He's yelling at me, telling me I'm a terrible employee. It never feels right. It seems real, and I can't escape it."

Larry didn't look at me and yanked out a roll of tape from a cardboard box. "Dreams mean nothing. I know you work your ass off at that job. Hicks is an old man. He doesn't say that stuff in real life, does he?"

"No. That's the weird part. Hicks is a mellow dude, mostly. He says weird things, but I never feel threatened."

"Don't worry about it. Too bad the dreams don't involve naked woman. Old, chubby Texans is not that hot."

I slapped Larry across the head, "Shut it. Nightmares can be spurred on by stress. You think my parents' divorce, paying for college, the allusive Sherry Lewis is causing it? I don't know. I'm no therapist."

"How are the folks?"

"Not sure. Every time I'm over there Kim is crying, and they pretend everything's okay. I know they yell a lot. Kim told me. I hate seeing them like this. I don't know why my dad is still in the house. The whole town knows my folks are headed for divorce. I think they're trying to save face."

"You ever find out what happened? Why they're getting divorced?"

"Tail on the side."

"Oh, shit. I was right. Your dad? He's such a straight-laced dude. Getting in the sack with middle-aged ladies?"

"I don't know her age. Some chick he met on a business trip. He's broken up over it. It was a onetime deal. I believe him."

"What was *that* conversation like? Awkward?"

"The worst. All I could think about was Dad all sweaty and making sex noises. I don't know if I'll ever recover. I still believe my parents only had sex twice. Once for me and once for Kim."

Larry shook his head in a mischievous manner thinking about what I said.

"Sick... asshole. You thinking about my dad having sex?"

"Nope. I'm thinking about your mom."

I gave no response.

"Actually, the rush of meeting a chick far from home, shacking up and flying home with a little secret, that's an idea for my next film."

"Okay, Kubrick. Why don't you think about something a little more important in the world? Like helping me cope with Sherry."

"What do you mean?"

"You met Chet, right? Well, he works at TB too. Sherry got blamed for those kids dying last summer. He believed Hicks was doing something shady behind the scenes to get the case dropped. Sherry got thrown under the bus and fired. He thinks there's more going on than meets the eye. It's dark."

"Ooh, woman of mystery. I like chicks with an edge."

"Back to earth, horn ball. This is serious. Sherry's getting set up."

"If it were me, I wouldn't get caught up in this stuff. It sounds like Sherry is trouble, Hicks is shady, and TB is a facade of fun. Do your work and don't get in with the wrong crowd. My opinion, amigo."

Larry was right. I knew avoiding the situation might be the right move. I didn't want to lose my job or put myself in harm's way. Still, I loved Sherry. She didn't know it, but I felt responsible, in a man defending his girl kind of way. Weird, I know. And I wanted no one else getting hurt or framed.

"I'll be safe. I don't want anyone hurt at TB. If it means going to the cops, I will."

"In horror movies the dude who tries to save the girl gets slaughtered with a saw. Don't be that guy."

I glanced out the kitchen window and caught portion of the Ferris wheel. It swayed in the morning breeze of the Pacific, and not a soul was on the pier. I wanted to know what happened at TB when the kid's died.

Was the Wheel something special?

Don't know, but it drew me in. I wanted to find out.

THE WEATHER WAS warm for October, and The Boardwalk was hopping with people. Families with small children, teenagers, and empty nesters walked the pier and enjoyed the weather and the amusements.

I was finding a rhythm on Dante's Hell. A crumpled piece of paper was taped to the control panel, my notes. Didn't want to forget the correct buttons to push and hoped to not kill anyone today.

I glanced at the paper as a casket lurched to a stop in front of the control booth. A kid no older than fourteen, with a face covered in lipstick, stumbled to the platform. I gave a nod like well-done young man. His girlfriend smiled and adjusted her skirt and wiped the corner of her mouth.

I remembered the dream of Sherry... and remembered it was only a dream.

Most days at TB consisted of the monkey-work of hitting buttons, pulling levers, and watching kids get to first base. Some people with smiles, some with terror in their eyes, and others bored. I didn't know if I bought in to selling dreams and inspiration like Hicks told us, but the job was fun, and better than cleaning grease from a fryer at Burger King. It was more enjoyable than expected. I had enough money to pay for classes in the fall at Oceanside Community. I took only part-time credits. The fall weather was good, and Bill needed more help at TB. I needed the money, and it worked in my favor. I was only taking general education credits and needed time to figure out a major.

Kelvin Rodriguez appeared out of nowhere wearing stock overalls and grease spread across his cheek. He played with a clipboard and wiped sweat from his forehead. He leaned over the control booth like he lost his keys. I focused on the ride and tried to ignore his snooping around.

"You need something?" I asked.

"Nope. Just ignore me. You're doing a great job, Neil. We like the loyalty you're showing at TB.

"Thanks. Just trying to live the Boardwalk Way," I said with a hint of sarcasm, hoping Kelvin didn't pick it up.

Kelvin smiled and wrote something on the clipboard, "Bill Hicks would like to see you after your shift. Please come by the office before you leave for the night."

I nodded.

Kelvin disappeared before I could ask for a reason.

My heart sank, as meeting the boss was never a good thing. I had only been on DH for a couple weeks and thought of all the reasons I could get fired. I showed up on time, dressed appropriately, and ran the ride with efficiency.

Once, I hit the red button on accident during a run. That's the emergency button which shuts the ride down and all the lights go on. A recorded voice says, "please follow The Boardwalk attendant to the nearest exit." You should've seen the kid who shit his pants next to his girlfriend. I imagine they never dated again.

But mostly, I kept my head down, and didn't get caught

up in the chatter about scandal and TB being haunted. Or whatever the latest rumor was.

An hour later a young man slipped in next to me at the control booth.

"How'd it go? Anything I need to know?"

Reggie Smith was a new employee and hired at the same time as me. He had red hair and freckles and could pass as Ron Howard's twin. Smith was a religious kid and often quoted Bible verses while working. I didn't mind. It was better than some of the other crude talk from other seasonal help. A little Jesus chatter was a nice change.

"Uneventful... except Kelvin called me to the boss's office. Say a prayer for me," I said.

Reggie nodded and folded his hands in prayer, "I did... in my heart. Blessings with Hicks. If God is for you who can be against you?"

"Huh?"

"It's Romans... never mind," Reggie said.

I waved goodbye and made the journey to Hicks' office.

I played all the reasons in my head of why Hicks wanted to see me. After my parents divorced, I felt a compulsion to please Bill. I don't know if he'd taken on a father figure role, because my own dad was living in his head and had trouble being present. I wanted Bill to be happy with me like I wanted my dad to be happy when I got an "A" in English. Not sure why. A therapist could sort me out.

I walked out of DH, passed Sea Lion Flyer, right at One Ball, and straight past Whirly Bird, the spinning ride guaranteed to make you puke. Hicks' office sat behind WB with a discreet door that read "Employees Only." Only a handful of people even knew where the office was. It was always invite only.

A wooden door, with hand painted TB logo of the pier and Ferris wheel in the background, greeted my eyes. I knocked and took a deep breath.

No response.

I breathed in deep again, knocked and pressed on the unlocked door. It slid open.

The smell of burning incense and other strange noises came from the back. The lights were turned down, and I heard rustling and thumping coming from what appeared to be an office.

I crept in feeling like I didn't want to disturb whatever was going on in the office. It felt important. The noises grew louder and sounded like chants of intelligible words. I stepped into the room a little deeper and pulled back a door that was cracked open.

A man was hopping around and chanting with incense rising to the ceiling of the brown paneled office.

Bill Hicks was doing what appeared to be a rain dance, dressed with what appeared to be an authentic Native headdress. The one he wore at employee orientation. A long brown skin with hand drawings of bison, tepees, and other indistinguishable objects hung loosely around his frame. I'd hoped all the garb Hicks wore didn't offend Native Americans. I wouldn't know.

My watch told me I was a couple minutes early. Hicks didn't tolerate being late for meetings or anything. I stood back and shielded myself with the door. The show seemed to last a couple minutes.

I knocked on the door and pretended nothing happened.

Bill walked over to his desk and blew out the incense sitting on top. He laid his headdress on a chair in the corner and caught his breath for a second. He walked right toward me, and I didn't know if he knew I was in the room.

"Take a seat partner. I've been expecting you," he said, wiping his nose with a Kleenex.

I didn't know if I should say something about the dance or keep my mouth shut, "Sorry to disturb you in that... little... dance... thingy."

Hicks lit up and smiled, knowing I didn't know what the hell I was talking about. "That little dance thingy was an authentic Sioux Sun Dance. I do it every day. That's why we've been having such good weather. I learned the dance when I lived on a reservation in North Dakota, for a summer in college."

I nodded and didn't know if I should tell him he's full of shit. Not the reservation in North Dakota part, but I don't think the warm weather at Sea Lion Beach was because of a Sioux Sun Dance. "That seems like a logical explanation. We're having some great weather, and business is booming regardless of the source."

Hicks said nothing, threw his boots on the desk, and leaned back in a swivel chair. "Business is good. TB's built on the back of kids like you. Without the loyalty and hard-working employees of this park, we're just a glorified kid's birthday party with scary clowns."

I raised an eyebrow not following the analogy, "You're lucky to have good people working here. I think we try hard to embody the Boardwalk Way."

Hicks paused a couple beats, and I could tell he was planning his next words. He leaned in close across the desk. "You're one of the good ones Neil. I know you've been through a lot with your parents' divorce. Yet, you work hard, show up every day with a good attitude, and embody TB Way, as you say."

"Thanks Bill. I've been through some stuff this summer, but working at TB has been a great opportunity and good therapy. It's been a lot of fun."

Hicks grinned and slapped me on the arm, "That's why I'm giving you a promotion partner."

I gave a crooked smile not because I was happy, but because of confusion, and didn't know what to say. Many TB employees had slaved for years with no promotion. I'd only worked a few weeks, and on DH for crying out loud. Not brain surgery. Monkey work.

"Bill, I'm flattered, not sure what to say."

"Say yes, son. Yes to the promotion."

"But... I don't think I need more responsibility. I'm just getting the hang of DH and want to do that well, before working another area of the park. Besides, things aren't good at home."

Bill landed his boots back on the ground and stared at me like I told him DH was not scary at all. "What did you say?"

"I don't need the promotion. Maybe there's someone else who could use it?"

"Are you shitting me boy? Where I come from you take what you get. You gonna tell me how to run my business?"

"No sir. I'd never tell you how to run TB. Honored to be considered for promotion. I just don't need the extra responsibility right now. Got a lot of stuff going on with college, parent drama, girlfriend trouble, and a roommate who thinks he's Stanley Kubrick," I said, nervously trying to convince Bill before getting fired.

Bill leaned across the desk and planted a finger in my chest and his eyes turned red as he growled, "I'm not asking you. I'm telling you you're getting this promotion. It starts on Monday."

This was a side of Bill Hicks that opened up like a Jack-in-the-box. I didn't know Bill's buttons, but the wrong ones just got pushed. I thought about all the people who needed the promotion more than me and the target now on my back. The new kid waltzes in and gets a promotion and pay raise after two weeks on the job. I imagined being strung up in the middle of the pier, like an old Western movie.

"Okay... I'm sorry, Bill. I'll start on Monday. Move some things around."

Bill didn't relent and stood hovering over me with a grin that was part nice and part evil, "In college I worked three jobs, married, and had a dog. Don't tell me you're busy. You don't know what busy is, son."

He sat back in the swivel chair and acted like he didn't just chew me out, "I'm so proud of you, Neil. You will shine bright in TB universe."

"You didn't tell me what the job is."

"Oh, how stupid of me. You'll keep running DH, but I want you to take part in the shows. Talk to Brock Thomasorrow. He'll set you up. They'll start you small, don't worry."

Dammit, I worried. The shows didn't feel like a promotion, more of a demotion. A stage was the place to vomit when giving lines in the school Christmas concert. I think that's why I liked the writing life. Quiet. Solitude. And no need to speak in front of living humans.

"Okay, Bill, sounds great."

Bill waved me away and placed the Indian headdress back on his head while saying, "We're done, partner. You're a bright and shining star. Keep it up. I need to bring down more good weather, if you know what I mean. Hear the money in the registers?"

I didn't hear the money but knew what he meant, and it

was weird. Something opened up that day, and Bill seemed to change. I had a new promotion and was not happy about it. The first college kid ever to not want more responsibility and money.

I had my reasons.

Brock Norris wore tight jeans, a derby hat, and a large mischievous grin. He was my new supervisor for *the shows*. Most people knew he was gay, but he'd never officially come out, at least to my knowledge. It wasn't popular in the 70's to make sexual identity public, especially if you weren't heterosexual.

Years later, I heard Brock was working on Broadway producing musical scores. Not surprising, as he was the most talented musician I ever met. He breathed song. Who knew he'd get his start at TB?

I sat in a director's chair watching Brock attach a black beard to my whisker-free face. He placed a top hat on my head and grinned.

"Perfect, sexy man. If you're not Abraham Lincoln, you sure as hell will pass as his twin brother."

I gave a forced smile, not wanting to channel the vibe of our sixteenth President. I wasn't happy about the new promotion and new responsibility of the shows. My mission was to stand up on The Starlight Theater stage and give the Gettysburg Address, not before the Star Spangled Banner finished playing. It was a patriotic nod to our country, which was fine. The only problem is no one cared. Drunk teenagers mocked the performers and threw trash at our feeble attempts in acting. An occasional old person would come, and I emphasize "occasional."

Brock wrapped a long, black coat over my shoulders, more like a cape, and took a step back to ensure everything was straight. "Whamo! Another Brock Norris creation. You're Abraham Lincoln incarnate. Remember, take your time on the speech. In rehearsal you were speedreading."

He didn't understand the nerves warring in my sThomasach. When I'm nervous words come out fast. I can turn a five-minute speech into two, ask my English teacher in high school. Public presentations were not my favorite day of the year.

"Anything else you suggest for not throwing up during the performance?" I asked, straightening my hat and wiping drips of sweat from my forehead.

Brock leaned in and grabbed my chin like my mother used to do before wiping boogers from my nose. "Pretend the audience is naked. My drama teacher in high school swore by this technique. I know it sounds corny, but it works. It'll slow your heart down and keep you calm. I'd like to see you nak-."

I held up my hands in surrender, "Whoa, easy there, Brock. We barely know each other."

Brock and I had a healthy back and forth, and he knew I wasn't gay, though he never admitted as much either. Despite deflecting the opposite sex like armor in battle. He figured I could use a companion... of any kind.

"Sorry, Neil. The theater gets my juices going."

"Speaking of juices. This weather is unbearably hot. How do I not pass out in the Lincoln suit?"

A heat wave came through California the week of my acting debut. I didn't want my beard to come off with the cheap glue holding it down and ruin the persona, as if anyone would even see the show. Yet it added to the nervousness.

Brock handed me a large plastic cup with a curly straw. "Drink this. I don't know what else to tell you. Theater is battle. You gotta fight to perform. And take breaks, and sit down when possible."

I nodded and took a deep drink and watched the water race through the curves of the straw. Brock's advice wouldn't help. I imagined passing out and Brock giving me mouth to mouth while stoners threw corndogs at me.

I had no clue why anyone at TB would want this job. No one liked the shows, and it was common knowledge. Was Hicks trying to punish me for something? I made a couple bucks extra, but the shows were the least favorite attraction at TB. Bill asked, more accurately told, me to do this. You don't cross Hicks as I was learning.

Kelvin Rodriquez opened the backstage door where Brock and I prepared for the show. He held the clipboard across his chest and gave me a deep stare that didn't exude hospitality.

"Heard you got a promotion," Kelvin probed.

Intrigued by the statement, I hesitated for a second. "Yep."

Kelvin had worked at TB for five years and never had a raise or promotion. That was at least the rumor in the employee breakroom. I could tell he was not happy with me.

"I know you're doing a good job. But raise and promotion after a couple weeks is not normal. You kissing Hicks ass?"

I shrugged, knowing kissing Hicks ass was impossible when I barely knew how to work a time card. Bill Hicks took a liking to me from day one. Never quite knew why. Maybe he felt sorry me because of my parents' divorce.

"No ass-kissing. I didn't want the promotion, but Hicks insisted. Working the shows is not my idea of fun," I said, pleading my case.

Rodriquez snickered. I didn't know if he thought the shows comment was true, or if my case was airtight. Maybe I was an ass-kisser? He tapped a pencil at the top of his clip-board, "You turned down a promotion? Hicks made you take it? That's a good one."

"Seriously. I knew other people deserved it more than me. He got in my face when I tried to get out of it."

"Really? The old man was in your face?"

"Yeah, he was bat-shit mad. Never seen him like that."

Rodriquez seemed to inch more onto my side and believe the story, "Hicks has many faces. You might've caught him on the wrong day. Wouldn't take it personally."

I didn't know how to hurry the conversation because the heat of my Abraham Lincoln costume was creating sweat running down my butt crack. I shook and wiggled my pants trying to get comfortable.

"Problems, chief?" Rodriguez asked.

"Costume is hot as hell. I got sweat in places that aren't supposed to be wet."

Rodriquez held off a laugh and covered his mouth, "I don't know if a promotion is worth it. That President suit looks terrible," he said, flicking my top hat with his pencil.

The mood of Rodriquez began to change, and thoughts of a pay raise didn't seem all that important for a moment. But I had my doubts about Rodriquez never getting promotions or pay raises. He was Hicks' right-hand man and spent more time with him than anyone at TB. I'm sure some money was exchanging between hands.

Rodriquez set the clipboard next to my stool. He furrowed his brow, and switched to a serious look like he was concerned about something. "The other day you asked if we knew each other. I lied. I knocked on your car window... and I dated Sherry."

A sense of relief came over me not because Rodriquez was a liar, but because I had spent days thinking I was crazy and losing my mind. I still had questions, "Why?"

Rodriquez hesitated, looked at Brock who was watching the entire drama with amusement, and then back at me. "I didn't like you. I was in a fragile spot after breaking up with Sherry. We still talked, and she mentioned you were interviewing for TB. I guess... I wanted to mess with you. Scare you off."

"I get it man, but you have nothing to worry about. Sherry and I aren't anything, just friends or something. It's confusing."

"I'm not worried about her. Sherry's in the past. She's had issues..."

"What kind of issues? Clicking jaw when she eats? Bad breath? What are we dealing with?"

"I don't want to speak bad about her. Just be careful man, whatever your situation is."

"When you knocked on my car window, that's what you meant when you said, 'Be safe.'"

He hesitated and pulled me to the side, away from Brock who continued to listen in "It's not only Sherry. Be safe at TB. Like I said, 'Things are not all they're cracked up to be.' Hicks is not all he seems on the surface. He has a good heart, but deep in every heart is evil, just saying."

"I thought you were just messing with me? You talking about the cover up?"

"Huh? What cover up?"

"Nothing," I said, retracting my words, "Is there something I need to know about TB?"

"There's..." Rodriquez didn't finish his sentence and grabbed his clipboard and ran out of the dressing room like someone saw him.

I didn't chase him as I was going on in a few minutes and needed to prepare and focus on the speech. But, to say I was confused, is an understatement. I didn't know *what* to believe or *who* to believe.

Brock slid in next to me and wiped a sweaty line from my face, "You ready superstar? That conversation seemed intense. Everything okay?"

"Rodriquez said this place isn't safe. What's your take?"

"Not much. Since those kids died last summer, there's been strange things happening."

"I hear that a lot. Like what? Why can't anyone tell the truth?"

"Easy, killer. Most of it's hearsay and unexplainable. You know, employees trying to get a rise out of each other on long, hot days at TB. I don't even believe in the supernatural. That's not for me."

"What do you mean? Rodriquez didn't say anything about the supernatural. This place haunted?"

"I don't think so... depends who you ask."

"You don't think so? I need answers Brock."

He rubbed my shoulder and tried to calm me down, "I wouldn't worry about it. You have a show to do. We can talk about it later. TB is a great place to work. I wouldn't listen to Rodriquez. He has his own issues."

"Like what?"

"You swear not to tell?"

I held out a pinky, "Pinky swear."

"The night those kids got killed, Rodriquez was hanging around the Ferris wheel flirting with Sherry. She needed a bathroom break. He took over the ride while she was gone. That's when the kids died. Everyone knows Sherry became the fall girl for it."

"That asshole. Why didn't he get in trouble? Didn't someone say anything?"

"There was a lot of confusion surrounding the deaths of those kids. When it happened Rodriquez threatened Sherry with her life if she told on him. He already had a rap sheet and didn't want to go back to jail."

"Is this common knowledge?"

"Depends who you ask."

"You so keep telling me."

"Some people think there's more going on."

"Like what?"

Brock leaned in and whispered, like someone was listening to our conversation, "Some people think Rodriquez and Hicks are doing something shady behind the scenes. Who knows what? They are quite chummy. Rodriguez is his right-hand man, and after the deaths he became a special assistant to Hicks. But no one knows it. He pretends to be a fix-it-guy and supervisor. That clipboard is a bunch of shit. He can't fix jack around here."

"Asshole. Giving me all that grief about the promotion. He's doing fine."

"Say nothing. All conjecture, Neil, and watercooler talk... if you know what I mean," Brock said.

I felt sick to my sThomasach. Didn't know if it was all this new information, heat stroke, or delivering the Gettysburg Address in a couple minutes.

Brock raised me to my feet and dusted off the long black coat. I wiped my brow and took a deep breath.

"You're a star. Remember, slow down the speech." Brock said, slapping me on the butt.

I stepped out from behind a curtain, introduced myself as Abraham Lincoln, and began the speech, "Four score and..."

The four people in the crowd included two stoners and two wide eyed elderly ladies. I rocked side to side and tried not to faint from heat stroke. I didn't know if it was the heat or the distrust of TB.

Who could I believe? Who could I trust?

My speech wasn't slow that's for sure.

THE SEA LION BEACH LIBRARY was sparse as I strolled long aisles of books and periodicals to feed my addiction. In a time with the popularity of TV, book reading was waning in 1979. I'd do my part and not let the new medium stranglehold the first love.

Interestingly, a passion for reading seemed to be hereditary. Dad read, Mom read, and even Kim read magazines.

In the backyard of the "Happiest Place on Earth" my Disneyland was the library, and continues to be so in old age. Escaping to faraway lands and considering the design of the universe were necessary for The Cancer. I needed books to keep me sane between rounds of chemotherapy.

Books were my savior when TB was becoming a hot mess. And when dates were nowhere to be found, an adventure with Thomas Sayer was just as good. Oh, sweet books.

I walked the aisles with no real strategy. I didn't care. The experience of book hunting was like treasure hunting. You had a map, sometimes, but the thrill of the find kept you going. In that moment, I needed a diversion to clear my head with all the shit going on at TB. Hicks seemed like a twofaced old man. Did he only care about money? Was The Boardwalk Way a farce? And what was up with his obsession with Native Americans? Hard to know.

Sherry's story seemed plausible. Was I blinded by her beauty and wanting a real date so much that she could tell me anything? Maybe. Larry was... Larry. The only sane one of the bunch which was hard to say out loud. Rodriguez might have slept with the boss in a nonromantic way. And I wasn't sleeping with anyone. The library was all I had.

Obsession with books began as a young kid on a farm. I didn't grow up on a farm, I'm a city kid. But, on long trips to Iowa to visit my grandparents on Dad's side, books were my arsenal for fighting boring car rides and incoherent conversations with my aging grandparents. If I ever heard, "Why don't you call Neil?" it'd be too soon.

My first taste of leaving the world and entering an alternative universe was Ray Bradbury's *Fahrenheit 452*. Once the Bradbury cherry popped it led to creepy thrillers from Jim Thompson, and hope-filled worlds with C.S. Lewis in *Chronicles of Narnia*.

At the end of a carousel of books I noticed a small sign with an advertisement. It was an exhibit on the fifth floor. Oceanside was celebrating 50 years as a city in California. They wanted to capture the history of its beginnings and speculate where it was headed in the future.

I left the first floor and climbed the stairs to the fifth. The exhibit was empty of people, and I looked around to make sure I was in the right place. It was the middle of the day and I enjoyed not having class or work at this time.

A glass case of newspapers showed former Mayor Robinson cutting a ribbon at the San Pedro Bridge. One city official smiled at the cameras at the opening of the Sea Lion Beach Library where I now stood. I enjoyed daydreaming about the times and places and history of our little city. It was where I grew up, and it didn't look like anything it once did fifty years earlier.

A photo caught my attention in particular. I smiled as I got closer, recognizing the individual. It was Bill Hicks shaking Mayor Robinson's hand at the groundbreaking of The Boardwalk. They both held shovels in their hands.

Inside I laughed knowing Bill never lifted a finger at TB. Let alone a shovel. He signed the checks and found cheap labor from Mexico for any building projects. At least that's what I heard.

I read the fine print under the photo. It said TB would change the fabric of Oceanside and bring many jobs and revenue for years to come, yet didn't say at the expense of tax payer dollars. Nothing is free; everything has a cost.

The last paragraphs of the article caught my attention. It said the project almost derailed when they discovered a potential Native American burial ground under the property. A group of Indians protested and tried to stop construction of TB. It didn't say the outcome.

I scratched my head, wondering the connection between Hicks' obsession with Indians and the TB project. A burial ground? Why in the hell would Indians be buried near the beach? How did all these pieces fit together?

I'm no private investigator, but that didn't stop me from wandering in circles trying to think through the pieces. I went back to the glass case and leaned over the photos, periodicals, and maps.

The left side housed a second photo of Hicks. He wore a Native headdress and stood in the middle of a group of Indians. The title said, "Local Business Man Supports California Natives."

Oh, shit. Was Hicks paying off Indians to keep them quiet over the Indian burial site?

I surprised myself that I'd even made this connection. Jumping to conclusions, of course.

I examined more of the photo. A man standing next to Hicks looked off. The young man wore a headdress, like Hicks, smiled, and was dark skinned. I figured he was Native American and part of the local community in Oceanside. But there was an eerie familiarity with the man.

Kelvin Rodriguez.

Hicks right-hand man. I stepped back from the case, grabbed my forehead, and felt the room spin. I didn't know who to believe, or what. Something was going down at TB. Why was Kelvin in the picture? Was Kelvin Native American?

Somebody needed to know my findings. I didn't know who, but somebody did.

An idea came from nowhere. I was in a library. What do you do in a library? Read... of course. You also research. My father told me new businesses registered with the city, before opening their doors. I wanted to see what TB was registered under. Make sure Bill Hicks was who he said he was.

I ran to the back of the library which housed city records and directories. An old lady sitting at a small desk read a newspaper. She looked up and was bothered by my presence.

"Can you help me with something?"

"Maybe. There's no porn in the vaults. Tell your little friends to stop bothering me."

"Excuse me?"

"Teenagers about your size come to this floor asking for

porn. I'm stopping you before you look like a fool. Go tell your friends."

I shook my head and couldn't believe what the plump gray haired old lady just said. Not a bad prank though. "No porn. I need to research a directory for businesses registered in the last couple of years. Can you help?"

The old lady lit up. She probably sat bored most days. This was also her Disneyland. "Oh, yes. What years are you looking for? I have every year since Oceanside became a city."

"How about... 1975-1978? I'll start there."

She darted to the back of the library and disappeared behind a glass door. I never saw an old lady move that fast. Black square heels clanking on the marble floors and her wide butt wobbling in time.

A few minutes later the librarian dashed back with a stack of books in her arms. The tower of directories almost toppled over on the table. "They're organized by business name or owner name, sometimes both. These are the three years you requested. If you need other years let me know," she said with delight.

I thanked the librarian and attempted to lift the large bounded books filled with hundreds of pages of names, numbers, and dates. A directory slipped off the top and slammed into the hard floors echoing through the library. A couple heads shot up reading quietly at tables. I raised a hand and mouthed "sorry."

An empty, round table sat in the left corner of the library. I flipped through the business directory and began with 1975. The directory for that year was large for a smaller city like Oceanside. I realized the directory also included the surrounding counties. This could take a while.

The Boardwalk opened a couple years ago, and 1975

seemed like a logical time for Hicks to register the new business.

I scanned with an index finger and mouthed the names of business and people. I searched Bill, William, Hicks, or something close. Found the name and looked to the right.

It said: "The Boardwalk. A Natives for California Company. June, 1975."

Natives for California? That didn't sound like Bill's business. I remembered him saying he started his first business in Texas with a different name. Why isn't Bill Hicks or his corporation on the registry? What in the hell is going on? I wanted information about the Natives for California.

The librarian made a copy of the page in the business directory. What was this going to prove? I wasn't heeding the advice of Larry, or Brock, in staying out of the mess. I was in the thick of the mess and not sure what to do next. Still, something was here, and I needed to know what.

Before I left, I asked the old librarian about the exhibit, "Is there a way to get a copy of a photo from the 50 Years of Oceanside celebration exhibit? I need it for a school project."

"Those photos are public domain and can be viewed by any card carrying member of the library," the librarian said, with a formal tone.

"Can you show me the one I need? Maybe where I can find it?"

I waddled with the librarian back to the fifth floor and showed her the articles of Bill Hicks' groundbreaking and the one with Kelvin and the Indians. She obliged and made a copy of both photos/articles.

So, I was armed with information that might either be coincidence, or enough to take down Hicks. I wanted to know which. Still not sure why I cared this much about a summer job. But people could be hurt. There was a mystery at TB to uncover and warranted a little more snooping around. It could explain what happened to Sherry. I didn't know at that point, but I needed to satisfy my curiosity.

The next person to find was Sherry. I wanted to question her and see what else she had on Hicks and TB, and maybe try to get another date. I'd be lying if I didn't think about the Fleetwood Mac concert at least five times a day.

This time I hoped for a real kiss, not a dream.

THE MOON HUNG full over Sea Lion Beach and made the stretching waters glisten along the Pacific. I picked at a mound of sand waiting for Sherry with a prepared set of questions replaying in my head. I wanted truth and nothing less. If anyone knew something about Hicks and Rodriquez, it was her. I needed to know what the hell was going on.

A figure came out of the dark and kicked sand on my feet. I turned to the smiling woman, "How goes it hunky man?"

Why did she call me these names? We'd gone on one setup date, and I still didn't know where I stood. Not helping.

I shoved my overgrown hair behind my ear and tried to formulate words. "Oh, hey Sherry. I didn't see you. Thanks for coming on such short notice," I said.

"Shocked to get a call from you after the concert. I assumed we were just friends."

I brushed a hand through my hair, "What do you mean? Nothing happened at the concert."

"Exactly the point. You never tried to kiss me. I got the hint."

"What the hell? I got cold signals all night. I don't get you," I said, being sidetracked from the prepared questions in my mind. I wasn't interested in sorting out our dating relationship. Was there one? Who knew?

"Let me cut to the chase. There's concern about The Boardwalk. I've discovered information that's unsettling. No half-truths. I need all the truth, and I need one hundred percent honesty. I will ask you a couple questions..."

Sherry agreed, her face blank as she could sense the seriousness of my tone, "I'm always honest with you."

"Yeah? How about Kelvin Rodriquez? What's his story?"

Sherry stood with hands akimbo on her hips, not liking the accusatory tone. "What do you mean? I told you he was my boyfriend. He's an ass, and we broke up. What do you want to know?"

"Just like that? Nothing else to the story?"

"What is this? You're acting strange, Neil. What are you fishing for?"

I paced in a mini-circle through the sand and took the position of a lawyer. With raised finger I asked another question, "Do you know the ethnicity of said boyfriend Kelvin?"

Sherry shook her head and placed a hand over her face, embarrassed by the lawyer act. "Please tell me how this is relevant to our relationship?"

"Answer the question."

"Hispanic."

"You sure?"

"I don't know. Never asked to see a birth certificate. Why does it matter? I never met his family."

I scratched and caressed my chin, "So... You're telling me you dated a guy and never met his family? Sounds fishy."

"Not sure how race is a factor in my dating relationships. I've dated all kinds of guys. I didn't go out with Kelvin long. He never invited me over. What's the big deal?"

"You don't find it odd that you were never invited to meet his family?"

Sherry nodded and was uninterested in my questions. "Like I said, we didn't date long. Not every guy invites me to meet their mother."

"What if I told you Mr. Rodriquez wasn't Hispanic at all?"

Sherry lost more interest and shuffled sand with her feet and stared at the ground. She glanced up, "Wait, what? You're questioning the ethnic heritage of my ex-boyfriend? Why does this matter on any level?"

"Yes, I am. The ethnic heritage of said boyfriend is vital for a lot of things."

"Why do you keep saying 'said' boyfriend?"

"I don't know. That's beside the point."

"Then what is he Sherlock?"

"I prefer Columbo," I said.

I pulled up the back of my T-shirt and removed a manila folder jammed in my jeans. Then I laid it open and removed a couple photos and handed one to Sherry, "Take a look. Please tell me what you see?"

Sherry held the photo and glanced up at me with eyes telling me to hurry, because her patience almost gone. I leaned in close and squinted because of the darkness of the beach.

"I see... Bill Hicks wearing an Indian headdress and

smiling in a group of Native Americans. He's obsessed with the Natives. Everyone knows that. What's the big deal."

I pointed to a man standing on the far right side of the picture. Asked Sherry to inspect.

"Who's that man?" I asked touching the photo.

Sherry squinted and held the picture almost touching her nose, "It looks like Kelvin. Why is he wearing an Indian headdress and standing next to Hicks?"

"That's a great question," I said, raising a finger. "Tell me what the caption reads under the photo?"

"Kachina 'Spirit Child' Begay receives check from local business man Bill Hicks."

Sherry's mouth widened as she took a second look at the photo, "What in the hell does this mean? Kelvin's not who he says he is?"

"Appears, so. I think your Hispanic ex-boyfriend is Native American. And his name isn't Kelvin, it's Spirit Child. You've been lied to. He's got explaining to do," I said, with a satisfying grin.

"What, do you think Kelvin... Spirit whatever... is getting a check from Hicks?"

"That's where this comes into play. What do you see?" I asked, handing Sherry another picture.

Sherry mouthed words and ran her finger along the type, "I see... Mayor Lewis and Bill Hicks cutting a ribbon with giant scissors. Looks like groundbreaking for The Boardwalk. Significance?" she asked.

"Big significance. Read the last paragraph under the photo."

"Again?"

"Read it now."

Sherry rolled her eyes.

She scanned the paragraph and read it aloud. She held

the photo at her side and glanced up at me with a puzzled look, "The Boardwalk sits on a Native burial ground? That might explain things."

"What do you mean?"

"I always felt TB had a weird vibe, like someone watches us. It might explain the strange happenings. The dead kids ..."

"You think dead Natives are causing all the problems? You believe TB's haunted?"

"I'll believe anything right now. No one ever has answers for anything. When the kids died, I became the scapegoat and was sent to an institution. No evidence and no explanation. Haunted, maybe." Sherry said, almost shocked she told someone in public about her time in a mental institution. "You want to date a crazy person?"

I waved her off and didn't care about that right then. I needed more about TB. "Before we talk about *the crazy*," I started, "I want you to examine one more document." I handed Sherry the photocopy of the business directory.

She scanned the page with her finger. "What's 'Natives for California Company?'"

"That's the question of the day. You saw Hicks' name, right? Let's put two and two together."

Sherry was losing interest, and I didn't know if it was the nut house, my flood of questions, or the lawyer act.

"Fine," she said.

"Hicks is obsessed with Natives. Not sure why, yet? Kelvin is Spirit Child... or whatever we're supposed to call him. And finally, The Boardwalk sits on a burial ground. The theme park we love to hate would almost vanish from existence, I'm assuming, if Hicks didn't pay off a local Native organization. From what I read, laws still protect

Native lands, unless they're willing to give it up. You follow?" I asked.

"I think so... Hicks paid them off? Just so TB could be built? That sounds wrong."

"I think so, but I don't understand his obsession with the Natives. That seems to go further back than a couple years."

"How do you know?"

"I walked in on him doing a Sun Dance. He mentioned during college he visited an Indian Reservation. I think in the Dakotas. Not sure what it means. He said little else."

Sherry bit her lip contemplating all the revelations. A wave crashed, and she leapt into my arms.

I caught her awkwardly and tried to not let her fall to the sand, "You okay?" I asked.

"Yeah, the wave scared me," she said, pushing me away.

Sherry became quiet and I could tell she wanted to leave or say something. "Neil, I don't think we should get involved..."

"You and me?"

"With all the Native stuff. I'm scared. The last time I told the truth, it bit me in the ass. I ended up in a looney bin, unemployed, with the people of Oceanside calling me a child killer. I might be a lot of things, but I ain't a killer."

Sherry choked up with tears. The weight of the night caught up with her. Maybe the weight of the last year. I wanted to push further but not sure how far. She answered it for me.

"You need to know more. One hundred percent truth, right? I'm giving it to you."

I nodded toward Sherry to go ahead.

"Hicks paid me off..." she said, convulsing in tears, hands covering her face. "I'm not a liar. I wanted to tell the truth. But no one was protecting me. No one would believe a twenty-one-year old girl over Hicks. He told me if I didn't lie… he'd hurt me."

"Hicks said that?"

She nodded, "He's an evil man."

"Seems to be the case."

Sherry wiped her nose, "We needed to survive. My mom lost her job and Dad ran out. I needed money and it blinded my judgment. I guess we all have a price."

"What did he pay you for? What secret was he hiding?"

Sherry wiped double tracks of tears running down her face and tried to compose herself, "The night of the deaths, I was working the Wheel. I needed to pee after working four hours straight. Kelvin, Spirit Child, came over and flirted with me. He said he'd watch the ride until I got back. When I was gone, those kids we're killed. I had no idea. I got caught holding the controls and the blame. Hicks got wind Kelvin was working when they died. Don't know who told, but Hicks didn't want him to fall. I became the fall guy."

"It's all so confusing. The story in the paper made little sense. The trial thrown out for lack of evidence. Employees at TB and witnesses had different versions of what happened that night."

"You don't believe me, do you?"

I nodded and placed a hand on her shoulder. "I want to. I just don't know how Kelvin could've gotten away with this so… easily. Someone must of saw him, other than you, right?"

"Who knows? The irony is the money wasn't much and is running out fast. It's hard to find decent work with your face splashed across the front page for a murder trial."

"But you're innocent, right? Trial thrown out for lack of evidence?" I asked.

"I guess guilty until proven innocent. Death by association. I don't know. This town has shown little grace. I even sent an apology letter to the families."

"Damn. This is a hot mess. I still want to know what happened that night. There's more than meets the eye."

"What are you going to do, Sherlock?"

"Columbo," I said.

"Sorry."

"I don't know. But someone needs to do something. Talk to the police?"

Sherry shot out of her skin and pushed her hands in my chest. "Don't go to the cops. Hicks will know, and it'll get worse. I want to put it behind me. Please don't. Please don't."

I raised a hand in surrender and thanked Sherry for the time, then leaned in for a peck on the cheek.

She backed away and disappeared into the night.

I knew one thing for certain, We weren't a thing. Or were we? That summarized the story of '79.

The makeshift hammock swung with the late fall breezes of Sea Lion Beach. Our deck at the Roach Motel apartment was neglected with the busyness of work and school. Not now, though, I had a few minutes to read and escape while Larry was attended a class at UCLA's Film School. Space, free from Larry's chattering about the latest film, was a welcomed companion. A two-day seminar teaching the fundamentals of directing also gave me time to clean our dust bowl.

I flipped through the worn pages of *Huckleberry Finn.* Mark Twain's descriptions of life in the South made me want to escape. I dreamed of a slower pace and a different time. My parents thought I was born in the wrong generation, an old soul of sorts.

The pages of the novel blew over with the cool breeze. I imagined writing the next great American novel. Bulbs flashed as I took the podium to receive the Nobel Peace Prize for Literature. I made the speech and dedicated the book to Sherry.

I shook off the dream and came back to reality. There's

no money in writing high literature. I'd write something commercial like Stephen King's *Carrie*. That seemed to pay the bills just fine. I'd need to feed my family someday. People wanted entertainment and didn't want to think about anything that matters.

I flipped another page and watched the sun rise high in the East. I had to work later, but couldn't sleep, so got up at 6 AM. I thought about Sherry and the beach, mostly thinking about Hicks and Kelvin, Spirit Child, or whatever we should call him. I thought about the lies Hicks told me and the team, with the infamous Boardwalk Way speech. The stuff about service and family didn't carry the weight it did before. He only cared about the botThomas line and keeping his name clear. A movie played in my mind of what I'd say to them. But, I knew deep down I wasn't the fighting type. Maybe I needed to heed the advice of Sherry and stay out of it.

I set Huck Finn down and gave a sigh.

Sherry backed up when I tried to kiss her. I never was good at reading signals.

A seagull gave out a cry, and a bicycler waved a hand on a morning ride. Sea Lion Beach was a peaceful place despite the mess lurking hundreds of yards away at TB. I didn't want to quit. The people at TB were kind, and a bad seed in the batch shouldn't force me out.

Why was Hicks confusing? You wanted to believe him. Maybe it was the Texas drawl that brought down inhibitions and end with people hanging on every word. Accents do that.

I wanted to believe Sherry, yet something still held me back. I wanted to give her the benefit of the doubt. She had good reason to take the money from Hicks. Still, the whole thing seemed off.

I leaned back in the hammock letting my brain take a break. My eyes fluttered, then closed, before a tap on my shoulder shot me awake. I jumped and threw the book on the ground.

"Sorry, kid. I'm getting in my route early this morning," said the mailman handing me a pile of bills, magazines, and a small envelope.

I thanked the mailman who disappeared down the beach and sorted the bills to the right by tossing them on the ground. I hate bills. I made a second pile for Larry's ten magazines, all relating to film and pop culture of course. I was convinced all his extra income, if any, went to magazine subscriptions. Then, I chucked the junk mail over my shoulder and noticed the small envelope.

Larry and I never got letters. I slid my finger under the small envelope and looked for a return address. None.

Our address handwritten and appeared to be from a girl. Too neat. No way it would pass for a dude I knew.

I scanned the yellow, college ruled paper:

Dear Neil,

I hope this letter finds you well. I know we've had a confusing relationship this summer. Sometimes I don't know how to say what I really want to say.

I held the letter to side and shook my head. You think? I kept reading:

·   ·   ·

Maybe a letter would be the best way to explain myself. Things have been hard, for me and my family, as you know. I have responsibilities most people our age shouldn't. We should work, go to school, concerts, parties, and hanging out with friends on the beach. I'm forced to deal with unemployment, taking care of my family, and dealing with all the shit from The Boardwalk.

I wish I were more of a fighter. To fight for the things you know are right and good. I'm not.

I think you're one of the kindest, sweetest, and funniest guys I've ever met. I'll forever cherish our shower at The Snack Shack, the Fleetwood Mac concert, and talks on the beach. I wish we could've met under different circumstances.

I'm going away with my family for a while. We're moving from Oceanside and finding cheaper living in the Midwest. I hope the new beginnings will be good for my family.

The summer of '79 will always be in my heart. Please understand and all the best.

XOXO,

Sherry Lewis

I threw the letter in the air and watched it flutter to the ground.

"That bitch. She's leaving? All the time and effort to make things work, and she bails. Figures. You're right Sherry Lewis. You are not a fighter. I'm more of a fighter and that ain't saying much. Could the letter be any more confusing?"

The rational part of me knew what Sherry was doing was noble. Her family was struggling, and the new situation would be good. But my heart, that love and longing part, didn't want to see her go. I didn't know where we stood, and still I wanted another shot. I didn't know what to think or feel. I wondered if what hung over her head from TB was too much. Maybe the Midwest was what she needed? Who knew? Now I was stuck knowing what I knew and Sherry sgone forever.

I picked up the letter and examined closely, like it was a forgery. Even smelled it. A hint of cherry lip gloss. Oh, those lips.

I went inside, placed the letter on the table, and showered needing to figure out how to face Spirit Child and Hicks.

Work would suck today. That's the first time all summer.

I FINISHED my shift dodging Spirit Child and Hicks, not ready to face them knowing what I knew. Besides, what would I say? "Excuse me, I think you're paying off witnesses and Native American organizations under the table. Is this true?"

The Boardwalk was a good job while transitioning from high school to college and the real world. I needed to play nice a little longer before opening the hornet's nest. If there was one.

My shift flew by on the Wheel. I watched the slow turns and couldn't shake Sherry from my mind. She was hurting. Her family was hurting. I just couldn't believe she was gone forever.

When times in life got weird Dad always had something wise to say. I needed a listening ear and wasn't sure if anyone was safe to open up to.

Dad and Mom were trying to make due under the same roof. He was unfaithful and stuck around for a time. Never understood that, but he was a good man and hard to stay mad at for long. Maybe they'd make it work.

I knocked on the door of his office and poked my head around the corner. He sat slouched in an overstuffed leather chair reading under a gold lamp. He lowered his glasses and smiled when he saw me, "Son, how the heck are you? Come in grab a seat." He pointed to a second leather chair.

The side table was piled high with books. My love of books began in that study.

I ripped the book he was reading from his hands and scanned the title. Stephen King's *The Shining*.

He gave a crooked smile.

"King? That's not typical for you."

Dad looked embarrassed like he'd been caught with a *Playboy*. He read science, history, engineering, and mathematics. Such mainstream fiction never littered the walls of his books.

He covered his mouth and whispered, "It's superb. When things happened with Mom, I needed breezy reading. Some friends recommended fiction. I now understand Jack's craziness, if you know what I mean?"

I nodded and placed the book back on the table and prepared my words, "I'm glad to see your literary tastes expanding. Just read *Carrie* again and loved it."

He nodded and put his glasses at the bridge of his nose, "What's on your mind, kid?"

The question brushed by my ear as I admired the high shelves of books smiling on the wall. There must've been a thousand titles. I considered my dad a learned man, always looking for a new angle, idea, and escape. He wanted to explore the deep mysteries of the universe. I often wondered if his infidelity rooted in wanting to experience something new and fresh. An affair was not a wise choice. Still, I knew the feeling of needing something new and exciting. Life gets mundane, and we stop smelling the roses.

My dad tapped me on the shoulder and awoke me from the book coma. "You were saying, Neil?"

"Oh, yeah. I'm stressed at work right now. Dealing with a couple challenging employees at The Boardwalk. Nothing big."

He nodded and took a sip of a brown drink in a short glass, "Big enough to come here. I haven't seen you around in a while."

I nodded and stayed silent.

"I get it. Life's full of adventure and old Dad gets leftovers. I understand. But the good news is I worked thirty years with many of the same people. Difficult ones. Cranky ones. And people I wanted to toss off Oceanside Bridge."

I laughed.

"What would you do if you knew something... was off... and wanted to make sure your information was correct, before saying something?" I asked.

Dad could tell I was grasping for words and holding back, "Can you explain what you mean?"

"Yeah, maybe. Remember when I had that project in Intro to Business class senior year? We had to research local businesses and find out revenue versus expenses for the year. We went to the library and looked up a couple of those directories."

He chewed at the corner of his black rimmed glasses and thought for a second, "Oh... yeah. That was great fun. We talked to the owner of *Freddy's Flowers* and the Italian restaurant. What was it, *Mario's*?"

"Yep, got it."

"I remember they did well that year and were way in the black. Surprised because the lasagna at Mario's wasn't good, if I recall," he said and then winked.

Steel trap. My father could remember inconsequential

details from thirty years ago. All I remember is I passed the class.

"You're the one who told me about the business directories at the library. How reliable do you think they are?"

"If your business is not in the directory, you can't operate in Oceanside. I don't see how someone could fudge on information. Suppose it happened a time or two. Why?"

"Oh, nothing. Another school project. I want to ensure my research is accurate. It's a big part of our grade."

"Sounds interesting. What class?"

"It's, well, ugh, for a business class. We're researching local businesses and asking a simple question: 'What is the correlation of longevity and success for businesses thirty years and older.' It's a dumb elective course."

He gave me a puzzled look, like he knew I was lying. I hated everything related to math, business, or science. Too exact of a discipline. I liked the fluidity of English and language arts.

"Okay... that seems like a question a professor could answer. Have you asked him or her?"

"Not, yet. Sometimes these community college profs aren't great. I wanted to double-check with a trusted source."

Dad smiled, "How are classes going?"

"Fine. I'm going part time this semester. Working a lot at The Boardwalk. Need to make money."

"I like a man with a plan. When I was your age, I worked and went to school. That's the way it was. I think paying for college as you go is wise."

No matter what, my dad always supported me. I could tell him I was collecting cans to pay for college and he'd say, "Way to go. Keep it up."

Don't know if I succeeded, but it's the dad I tried to be

to my three kids. Support them, correct if needed, and always love. Even if they act nuts.

"Let me ask another question."

"Shoot. I need more of a challenge," he said, sipping on his glass.

"What if... while researching, you find a business is doing illegal things? Hypothetically?"

"What kind of illegal things?"

"Oh, I don't know. Just bad things."

"If I knew a company was into something bad. I'd go to the police, I guess. Why?"

"No reason. In the business world, people often do bad things behind the scenes. Remember when Dudley Corporation sold fake stocks to their employees?"

"Yes, I do. It made national news for Oceanside. There something you want to tell me?"

"No, just hypotheticals. It's something we're studying in business ethics."

I slumped in the chair and avoided eye contact. I followed with more questions, "What if... you worked at a place and thought illegal things were going down but couldn't prove it? What would you do then?"

My dad leaned back in the chair, rubbed at his chin, and looked back at me. "These questions are strange. You care a lot about business ethics, I see. But if it were me, I'd not say anything until you knew for certain. I'm more of a facts guy, not assumptions. That's why I enjoyed being an engineer for thirty years. You need facts, not conjecture," he said with a confident grin.

"Facts, not assumptions. That's reasonable. I wouldn't want to get anyone in trouble that didn't deserve it. Is that what I hear you saying?"

"This sounds personal. You sure there's nothing you want to tell me?"

"Nope. I'm learning a ton about business ethics and wanted to hear your take, on ethics that is."

My dad sipped his brown liquid, and I could see satisfaction with each drink. This was a new thing for me. He never drank, at least not in front of the kids. Family policy with a history of drunks in the lineage.

"So, how's the job? You still like working at The Boardwalk?"

I paused, knowing things were confusing right now and my dad could see it in my face. "It's okay. Working with the public has its ups and downs. Employees that don't always tell the truth. You know, typical work stuff."

He nodded and sipped, and I could tell he wanted to say something wise. He had that look, and always involved rubbing his chin. A tell. "When I came up through Texaco, there was a manager that rubbed me the wrong way. I was a young kid, not much older than you, and doing an internship in one of their offices. Every day he'd get on my case, and I never knew why. I showed up on time. Worked hard. There was no reason to get after me, but he did. I didn't like it and didn't know what to do. Anyway, time went on, day after day, same crap. Then one day I called him out. I told him the way he was treating me was unfair."

I interjected, "What happened?"

"He stopped being an asshole." I could tell the alcohol was kicking in because Dad never cussed. Maybe this was a new thing, too.

"Really? Just like that?"

"Yep," he said, finishing the last sip of brown liquor.

I paused a couple beats and leaned in the leather chair

and thought about confronting Hicks. It scared the shit out of me, and I didn't think it would go as easily as my dad made it sound. I needed the job, the money, and yet, I wanted to do the right thing. Of coure, I wasn't sure what the right thing was when my information was a tangled mess.

Dad leaned in close, and I could smell the Bourbon, or some kind of hard liquor on his breath. "Turns out my angry manager was stealing money from the company. Writing off personal expenses as company ones. He was living a lie and took it out on me. Be careful with people. Everyone has a story. You never know what you might find behind the curtains."

I reflected on how Hicks was getting angry with me the other day in his office. Around TB, he was pushing me hard and getting upset over little things. When I dropped my gum wrapper on the landing of Dante's Hell, I thought he would punch me in the head. He was steaming mad. He gave me a lecture on cleanliness leading to godliness, or some shit. I tuned out after a while because people were staring at us, waiting in line. Maybe the Indian stuff, the lies, and payoffs were all true. He was the liar and mad because he couldn't deal with his own conscious. There's a story behind everyone's story.

This made sense.

I rose to my feet and stretched out my arms as it was approaching midnight. I had worked all day and needed to get sleep. Dad didn't seem to want to acknowledge the realities of the divorce and the drinking and cussing. I didn't have the energy to go down that road. Nevertheless, I always appreciated his fatherly wisdom, and he seemed to be timely and right.

I hugged him around the neck and kissed his cheek, "I

love you, Dad. Everything will work out. Thanks for the chat."

I leaned back and could see his face welling up with tears. "I loved her so much..."

We didn't need to say anything. Love is a complex thing.

HEATHER RILEY WORKED on DH with me that day. I pushed buttons, watching the casket come to a stop not paying attention. My mind wandered and queasiness settled in my sThomasach.

She waved a group of kids onto the ride, glanced at the controls, and gave me an eye, "You okay, kid? Someone needs to tell your face it's not a funeral."

I didn't speak, nodded, and gave a fake smile.

"You look like someone pissed in your lemonade. You sure nothing wrong?"

Riley, as we called her, was one of my favorite employees during my time at TB. She grew up in the South and used the funniest southern lingo. If we worked together, I spent most the shift needing translation. I wasn't laughing this day.

Her dad transferred to California because of the military. He served in the Marine Corps at Twentynine Palms, worked in 7th battalion tank patrol. Tough dude.

"I got girl troubles," I said, pressing a flashing green button on the control panel of DH and stared off into space.

"What kind of trouble? That one girl you always talking 'bout, Sharon?"

"Sherry."

"Sha break your balls?"

"Huh? What's a 'Sha?'"

"Expression we use in Louisiana. Your honey, baby, dear. Sha's break the balls of men all the time. Crush their will to live. It's what we do. You need something to eat or drink? By the looks of it, she done you bad."

"I'll be fine. Haven't been sleeping much last couple of nights. I thought, no big deal when I got the letter. Never knew where we stood. Sherry's confusing. But the letter messed me up. I want to reconcile things with her and kill her at the same time. Sha busted my balls good, right?"

Heather nodded and tapped my shoulder with a tender hand, "That Sha done left you a letter. The worst. What did it say?"

I slapped a button on the control panel and gave a half smile to a passenger, "Oh, you know. How great I was. Sorry for not being able to express herself. And, she's moving to the Midwest. This Sha broke my balls and stepped on them for good measure."

"Ouch. Why the need to tell a guy how great they are? If they so great... why leave?" Heather said, with a grin.

"Exactly! It makes no damn sense."

"You must've left the pig pen open. Let the wolves in."

I scratched my head. "Is that a Louisiana saying?"

"No. I used to get in trouble for leaving the pig pen open. Wolves come in and eat em'. What'd you do for Sherry to leave California?" Heather asked, waving a hand-holding couple into a casket.

She smiled at a blonde kid who sat down in the casket. "I know what they're gonna do," she said, glancing up at me.

I slapped at buttons not focused on the job. "I didn't do nothing wrong, I think. All I wanted was a kiss. Didn't happen. The story of my life. Nice guy, try to be helpful, and it always backfires."

"Settle down. There's more crawfish in the creek. Girls want someone with an edge. Not no cry babies. Maybe try bad guy instead of good guy approach."

"Maybe. But, the only guys I know who have an edge, are assholes. Like Kelvin..."

"Supervisor, Kelvin. He seems like a good guy."

"Don't let your eyes deceive you. He's not who you think he is."

"What you mean?"

"It doesn't matter. The point is, I am who I am. If girls don't like me for me, screw them."

Heather pulled a lap bar off a casket and helped an older woman onto the platform, "Easy, killer. I'm just saying, you don't always have to play it safe. Be more aggressive. You have a lot going for you. Good looking California, *Sha*. Steady job. Maybe show a different side."

I nodded at the advice ignoring a blinking red light on the control panel, "Ok. But, what does that mean? Do I need to ride a Harley and own a gun? Tell me what to do?"

Heather laughed, "I imagined you toting a pistol and riding a Harley. Not, pretty. That's not what I mean. You need to show a girl you want em'. You'll protect em'. Fight for them even when they reject you. That's a real man."

My life story is about not fighting for what I want, whether fear of sharing my writings with others or asking a girl to prom. I knew Heather was right about the fight. I wondered if my father had fought hard enough to get Mom back.

"You saying I'm not a man? Did Sherry leave because I didn't fight?"

"I don't know your situation, kid. I only speak from what I think Sha's want. We want fighters."

I thought about the Harley and imagined leather chaps with Sherry on the back.

The control panel lit up with flashing red lights. I wasn't paying attention to the warnings. A casket screamed down the tunnel to final resting spot near the platform. I came to my senses realizing the red lights were telling me to hit the brakes.

Front casket came to a screaming halt. A blonde kid with lipstick covering his face slammed his chin against black padding on the front of the casket. Blood exploded from his chin and nose. The kid slumped to the side giving out a scream. His girlfriend seeing the blood did the same.

Heather and I jumped into the car to pull him up and assess the situation.

"Dammit. I'm so sorry," I said, holding the young man's head back, and wiping off blood with a rag.

He tried to speak through the blood and the rag over his face muttering curses and incoherent words and being consoled by his make out partner for a few minutes. After she told him it didn't look too bad, he finally stood up and managed, "What the hell are you doing? We could've gotten killed, asshole. I want to speak to your manager."

Heather negotiated, knowing speaking with Hicks not an option. Employees ending up in his office because of unsatisfied cusThomasers are looking for work at Taco Bell or Burger King within a week.

"Please, sir. We're very sorry, and we'll make this right," Heather said, pulling out a ticket from the back of her blue pants.

The boy examined the ticket with a TB logo on front. "This is a free, day pass. You have access to the entire park for a day. On the house. Any ride, or game, on us."

Day Pass, the get-out-of-jail-free card for TB employees. Used sparingly, equivalent of breaking glass in an emergency. This was time to break glass. We only had five tickets available each month. CusThomaser are always right, according to Hicks.

The young man released the rag from his bloody nose and scanned the card, "This is cool. Can my girlfriend get one?"

Heather already used her pass. I looked at her and pulled one from my pocket. I knew two passes in one week wouldn't look good for her. Hicks would lose his mind.

"Here's another one," I said, handing the kid my ticket.

Heather peeked over and mouthed the words "thank you" and gave a smile. She knew I saved her ass, and might've saved both of our asses from a visit to Hicks' office. It was my fault, and I needed to own it.

Heather raised the lap bar from the casket and helped the kid and girlfriend onto the platform. She pointed them down the walkway, "Once again, we are sorry. Please take these passes and enjoy the rest of your day. The First Aid area is between the Ferris wheel and Sea Lion Flyer. Stop in if you need more help. They'll get you ice and Tylenol, if needed."

The couple waved and skipped out of sight as if nothing happened, happy to spend an entire day on us. I looked at Heather who was throwing the bloody rag away in a can. She gave a sigh and slapped me on the arm, "What the hell, kid. Pay attention. You gonna hurt someone a lot worse next time."

"I know. My mind's all over the place. I need a nap. Sorry."

"Thanks for using your Day Pass. You might've saved my butt on that one. Please, get your head right about the Sha. It's affecting your work."

"You saved my butt. I owe you. This job is shitty lately, but I need it. Getting my head right about Sherry is now top priority. That's the truth."

Heather and I finished chatting and realized we needed to get back to work as a group of people formed a mob. "Can we ride, or not?" A group of horny teenagers glared in our direction.

I jumped in the control booth and made sure all the lights flashed green. Heather took her spot on the platform and helped teenagers into their caskets.

I glanced up and felt a presence. Kelvin stood next to me, appearing seemingly out of nowhere. He held the clip board. My heart skipped a beat, "Hey, Kelvin. What you doing over here?"

He tapped the clipboard with a pen and gave a stern look, "Heard about a situation a few minutes ago. You want to share?"

I stumbled over words and tried to make something up, "Not sure what you're talking about. A kid might've bumped his nose on a casket. No biggie. It happens."

"It happens? How did it happen?" Kelvin said, now standing akimbo, awaiting an answer.

"Oh, you know, Casket came to a stop. Kid wasn't paying attention and slammed into the bumper. It happens all the time."

"All the time? We have safety measures that include kids not slamming their faces into caskets. I don't like the nonchalant attitude in this," Kelvin said, scribbling a note on the clipboard.

"Okay, not all the time. That would be crazy, right? I meant once in a blue moon. Hardly ever, one time I know of. Today's that blue moon."

Kelvin, agitated at my ramblings, scribbled something else on the clip board. "How many Day Passes you have left?"

"Not sure what you mean?"

"Show me your Day Passes."

I yanked passes from my pants and handed them to Kelvin, "I still have a couple. I might've given one away."

"Just now? Did you give one out just now?" Kelvin said, leaning closer to my face, and counting the cards.

"Yes. I gave one out."

Kelvin dropped his hands to the side and gave out a sigh, "Sorry to do this, Neil. Hicks will need to see you."

"Come on. I still have passes left. Give me a break."

Kelvin stood silent.

I mumbled under my breath, "Dammit."

I needed my own casket to climb in at the moment.

TEXAS MEMORABILIA COVERED the walls of Hicks' office. There was a signed Dallas Cowboys' football, a drawing of the Alamo, and an Indian Chief standing stoic in front of a teepee. I examined the artifacts hoping to find dirt on him. Nothing.

I waited to be called back by the secretary, and the tension and awkwardness were the same as the time when I caught my boss in a Rain Dance.

I concocted a story of why I fell asleep at the wheel of Dante's Hell, why a young man smashed his face on the ride, and why I gave out a Day Pass. My story was leading me to an application at Burger King.

The old secretary, I think his wife, waved me into the back office. Hicks faced away from me, staring out a high window behind a cluttered, wooden desk. Spirit Child Rodriguez stood behind me holding the clipboard with arms folded. I waited for Hicks to speak.

"Built my companies on loyalty, hard work, and elbow grease. Not the sharpest pencil in the drawer, but I work harder than most," Hicks said, still facing away and eyeing something out the window.

I snuck into a hard wooden chair across from Hicks' desk and fiddled my thumbs, wondering when he might turn around.

"The Boardwalk's an answer to prayer. I prayed with my momma at age six God would allow me to do great things. Many people think building theme parks is a waste of time. They're not great things, noble things. "Hicks why waste your time," they tell me. I don't agree. Impact of theme parks on a community is immeasurable," he said, turning and leaning back into his swivel chair. Hicks placed his cowboy hat on the side of the desk and propped up his feet.

"Neil, I need loyal people to run my park, hardworking men to see dreams of little kids come to life. Hell, I need men, like yourself, that'll protect the integrity of the employees who run this place. Partner, you passed the test."

I glared at Hicks looking deep into his blue eyes not sure what he meant by "test." I turned back to Rodriguez who gave a half smile clearly pretending to like me for Hicks' sake.

"What test, might I ask?"

"Yesterday on Dante's Hell, you passed the loyalty test. A test seeing if you're a man who can handle more responsibility, support the dreams of the next generation."

I gave a puzzled look over to Hicks and scratched my head, "You know what happened, right?"

"Hell yeah, partner. Gave a kid a bloody nose. We saw the entire thing on the cameras."

"Cameras?" I asked.

"We have cameras all over The Boardwalk. Need to protect these grounds."

"I see."

"How do you think we keep people safe, and keep an eye on employees? Wish they were all loyal like you, Neil. They're not. Steal from me all the time."

There appears to be a giant eyeball hanging over the control panels of DH. Never knew what it did, until then.

"You've been watching me?"

"Listening, too."

"Wait? Isn't that illegal?"

"No, sir. You can do whatever you like if it's in the company bylaws. We have cameras and audio surveillance all over TB. All legal, all good," Hicks said, giving a smile to Rodriguez.

"Isn't that overkill? The park's not big."

"You'd be surprised what we see... and hear. Saw a kid trying to light a fire in the bathroom other day. Need to protect the assets of TB. Vital for the future of Oceanside."

The atmosphere in the room changed. The revealing of surveillance didn't feel like the family atmosphere Hicks preached. Invasion of privacy seemed far from homey.

"Think of it this way, if not for those cameras we'd not be talking. You wouldn't have passed the test, and not given more opportunity at TB."

"What test we talking about?"

Hicks slapped his knee and gave a laugh, "You know. When all the lights on the control panel of DH went haywire. You handled it well, son."

"I fell asleep at the controls. Going through some stuff and lost focus. It could've been worse."

"Don't know what you're going through, but the malfunction happened right here in the office," Hicks said, pulling a small device from his desk drawer and holding it up. Names of the rides at TB were labeled below each switch.

He pointed at one on the far right. "See this? That's Dante's Hell. I can control it right here from my desk," Hicks said, flipping the switch back and forth and giving a smile.

The fog in my brain lifted, and the reality of what Hicks explained came into focus. "Wait, you made the ride malfunction? That was a test?"

"Yes, sir. A test to see what you're made of. You passed. Congrats partner."

I replayed the kid's face slamming into the casket and blood exploding from his nostrils. "Did you see what happened?"

"Like I said, friend, it's all on video and audio," Hicks repeated in a robotic tone, not present in the room.

"That kid broke his nose. Not sure what kind of test I passed, but I didn't do my job. Keep the cusThomaser safe... rule #1."

Hicks waved me off and pretended the broken nose didn't matter, "Those things happen all the time. Theme parks are dangerous places. We had a fat lady turn an ankle, slipping on an AThomasic Berry Blast drink. Not a big deal. That's what insurance is for," he said, peaking over at Rodriguez, and giving him a thumbs up.

I rubbed the side of my face, not sure how the test was legitimate. Most jobs I'd be fired. "Why am I here? Smashed a guy's face, you say I've passed a test. If this was college, it'd be the best news ever. Fail the test and still pass the class. Sign me up."

Hicks leaned across the desk and cleared a path through stacked paperwork. He had the look he got when delivering a goofy analogy or sage wisdom, Texas-style of course. "It's not the trials that matter. How you respond to trials is the mark of a man. That's why you passed our test. We wanted to see how'd you do under pressure. How you'd take control of the situation, or not? You took lemons and made lemonade. That's the kind of man we want working at TB, lemonade-maker. You passed. Congratulations."

"What does this mean?" I asked.

"You're getting a second promotion. If I'm not mistaken it's a promotion to the ride of your dreams, the Ferris wheel."

I paused a beat and glanced at Hicks and then back at Rodriguez. I remembered my conversation with Sherry pertaining to strange happenings surrounding the ride. My encounter after the TB job interview came to mind. It didn't carry the allure it did weeks ago.

I stumbled out words, "Humbled again, sir. But, ugh, not sure if I want it enough. You gave me a promotion for the shows. Still getting the hang of DH. A promotion's unnecessary. Maybe Heather can take it? She's great."

Hicks tapped the desk with his fingers. I waited for the rage like last time I turned down a promotion. He went to a whisper and pleaded with me, "Heather can't handle The Wheel. I don't give anyone the opportunity to hold her controls, manage her power. A promotion on this ride is significant. She holds a special place in my heart. It's the first ride we installed at TB. The park wouldn't exist without her presence. Only loyal, hardworking, and competent employees like you, Neil."

Though flattered by the comments of loyalty, I still sensed something off in Hicks' tone. I'd never heard him speak this lovingly and gushingly over The Ferris wheel. I knew he had a weird, out of balance obsession with it, but this felt different.

"Well thanks, but I'm going to pass. After screwing up at DH, even if a test, I don't need extra stress. I barely can handle the shows, DH, and not to mention school, and lady problems. Speaking of lady problems, you guys hear Sherry Lewis moved away?"

The room went silent. Hicks looked at me, lip quivering. He looked back at Kelvin whose head shook side to side. "You're not chasing that skirt are you?"

"It's complicated. Thought we were a thing, but she moved out of state. Signal is loud and clear. Not the best moment of the summer. Do you know where she moved?"

Hicks tapped the desk and stared to the right of me not locking eyes and looking distraught. He pointed a finger at me. "You want to know disloyalty? Look at Sherry Lewis. Never bring up her name around me again, you hear?" Hicks said, wiping spit from the corner of his lip.

I obliged and felt Rodriguez's eyes blowing a hole in my back. "Did you know Rodriguez dated her?" I asked, pointing a thumb back at him still holding the clipboard.

Kelvin rolled his eyes.

"Yes. We talked about it. Issue solved long ago."

"What issue? Sherry's not an issue to be solved. She's a person. Do you guys know where she is?"

I felt the manila folder pressing on the back of my pants. I was looking for an opening to show Hicks and Rodriguez the photos. I wanted to expose these bastards of whatever shady stuff they were involved in.

Hicks rose and calmed after ranting about Sherry. "You'll start on The Ferris wheel Thomasorrow. Rodriguez will show you the ropes. Don't be late."

He didn't hear a word coming out of my mouth. His mind made up. My pleas against the promotion were for naught. Probably the first time in history of summer jobs someone tried to turn down a promotion, twice.

"Okay, I'll be there."

Hicks held out a floppy hand covered in sun spots, "Welcome to the inside. Glad you're part of the team."

I left the office.

I stood at the base of the Ferris wheel, ocean winds blowing my hair. I tried to process all that went down. "Inside," what the hell does that mean? I didn't want anything to do with these guys. I needed to figure out what was going on and where Sherry was.

Something wasn't right. Now I had to learn a new ride.

"COME INTO MY OFFICE, NEIL."

Hicks stood over me. It felt like I was two feet tall, and he was a giant. I stared up at him, and blood dripped from his mouth. I covered my face thinking he might attack.

"I own you. I own everyone at The Boardwalk. You're my puppet, partner..."

"No, please! I don't want to be your puppet. I want to be free!"

I awoke in a pool of sweat, drenching the back of my Star Wars T-shirt. Drool streamed from the corner of my mouth and soaked the pillow. I shot up in the bed to find my bearings and scanned the small bedroom.

It was all a dream. This same one awoke me many times in the summer of '79. It's one I have occasionally, even as an adult. It's hard to know when dreams are warnings or just the mind playing tricks. I think the circumstances of that summer made it a little of both.

I glanced to the left and stared through the bedroom window. Light from the moon cast shadows across the blankets. I scratched my head and balls, flipped off my Star

Wars sheets, and stumbled to the kitchen for a glass of water.

Larry hunched over a pile of papers at the kitchen table. I thought he was splicing film as usual, but it was a different project. He raised a magnifying glass above a paper. A desk lamp hovered, lighting up the messy piles.

"What are you doing? It's 3 AM. Cutting film for Kubrick to look at?"

Larry ignored my attempt at humor and didn't lift his head from the table to acknowledge my presence. He angled the magnifying glass to scan the piles of papers, "I can't sleep."

I wiped drool from my lip and looked over the papers spilled across the table. I picked one up. "Research? Next film?"

Larry would read newspaper clippings to get ideas for screenplays. He said it was a little filmmaker trick when searching for new ideas.

He nodded and wouldn't look up from the table staring intensely at one particular clipping, "I'm worried for you, kid. You've been acting strange."

I wiped sweat from my forehead and the residue of the nightmare caused my heart to race. Larry hadn't looked at me yet. I crouched in and tried to get a better angle. "Yeah, I know. Not the dream summer I imagined. Sherry left me a John Dear letter. Work is sucking balls. I'm sure Hicks and Rodriquez are going to kill me. My parents are getting divorced. My sister is, well, my sister. Only one half date all summer. Sucks major balls."

Larry glanced up with a raised eyebrow and waved to hear more. He set the magnifying glass to the side and leaned in the chair.

"Had that nightmare again. Hicks' mouth was full of

blood. It was like he was controlling me. It felt like a prison. I wanted out... wanted freedom. But, couldn't. It freaked me out, dude."

"From what you tell me about Hicks, your dreams might come true."

I crossed my arms, "Not funny. I'm freaking out and don't know what to do. I had a crazy Aunt who said we must listen to our dreams. What if Hicks wants to kill me?"

"I wouldn't listen to Aunt Cindy. She has nine cats and hasn't left the house in twenty years."

Larry handed me a newspaper article tattered around the edges. It looked like an old news story from decades ago, "Check this out."

"What's this?" I asked.

"I did a little research on my own, took matters into my own hands to help you out. Read the paragraph at the botThomas of the photo," Larry said, pointing to the tattered photo.

"In 1966, a group of archeologists discovered 13 people, mostly children, buried on the shores of Sea Lion Beach. The bodies were believed to be the first European settlers to California in the 18th century. Best estimates concur the children were attacked by Native Americans. European settlers and a couple of Native bodies were found at the burial site. In 1975, the land was purchased by Bill Hicks, a local businessman in Oceanside, located at Sea Lion Beach. Paranormal investigators claim strange noises and unexplainable happenings around the area of the burial site."

I placed the photo on the table and took a deep breath. Larry leaned in the chair with a smile.

"Does this explain things?"

"Maybe. I didn't tell you, but I felt a hand on my

shoulder after the interview for TB. Except no one was on the pier that day. Where'd you get this article?"

"Holy shit. You felt a hand and didn't tell me? That's going in the next movie."

I slapped Larry in the back of the head. "Not everything is a movie idea. Let's get serious. This isn't normal. Where'd you get the article?"

"Who knew the library had this stuff. I was cleaning the house and saw your folder. I did my homework."

"Wait, you cleaned?"

Larry nodded.

I said, "From my research, I discovered Hicks bought land for The Boardwalk on an Indian burial ground. I didn't know settlers and Natives were slaughtered. That's new to me. This might explain why Hicks is in bed with the Natives. They didn't want him building on their sacred ground. Maybe a cover up? He must've paid them off to make everyone happy and move The Boardwalk project ahead," I said, scratching my bed worn hair.

"Hard to know. If Hicks is obsessed with Indians, like you say. Why would the Indians care if he bought the land? The Natives killed those European settler kids. That's not a good look for their community. You'd think they wouldn't want to make a big stink about it to save face, no?"

"Sure, if you look at it from the white man's perspective. Who was here first? The settlers invaded the land of the Natives. I'm not saying murder is right, but the stuff we learned in high school was always slanted."

"So why would Hicks go to all the trouble? Why not just walk away, not deal with it, find different land? Could've bought land in Sunset Beach. He's got the money."

"I don't know. It doesn't add up. How could Hicks be sure the Natives wouldn't ask for money later? Or change their minds and want to shut down the park by making a stink over the burial grounds, claiming the white man stole their land... again? Why would Hicks take that risk? He's obsessed with Indians, true. But, he's obsessed with theme parks, and Ferris wheels even more. Maybe that's the answer to the question. He will do anything to make The Boardwalk happen. When you're passionate about something you gotta fight, so I've heard," I said, holding up the article and taking a second look.

Larry slid a second clipping on the table and tapped at it, "It gets better. Check this one."

"Looks like a mini-version of The Boardwalk. One small Ferris wheel, a couple games, a food place. What's this?" I asked.

"Read the name on the botThomas."

"Who's Ronnie Hicks?"

"Apparently, Hicks' younger brother. He attempted a version of The Boardwalk and it failed."

"What's the connection?"

"Don't know, yet. Seems odd Bill's younger brother would start a park like TB. Never heard of it around Oceanside. Wonder why it never got off the ground?"

"Hicks never mentioned a brother named Ronnie. He talked about his terrible father. Not much else," I said, scanning the second clipping.

I read the botThomas of the article, paused a couple beats, and held up a finger, "Holy shit! You'd didn't read far enough, Sherlock. It gives the reason Ronnie's park shut down. A kid was killed at the park. Two years after the opening of the park, 1968, the park closed. The causes of death were never proven."

I slammed the clipping on the table and the papers jumped up. "Ronnie opens a park. Kid's die. Bill opens a park. Kid's die. What in the hell is going on? Could it be related to the burial grounds? This is bizarre."

"I love a great horror movie like the next guy, but you don't believe in that stuff, do you?"

"I don't know. Everything that happened, and is happening around TB makes little sense. Kids dying at Ronnie's park goes unsolved. The two kids at TB goes unsolved. It's all surrounded with mystery. What the hell is going on?"

"We need to tell someone."

"Not yet. Might just be random circumstance. Let's not accuse anyone until we know more. Hicks and Rodriquez are acting strange. They're treating me like a buddy and told me I'm an "insider." Gave me a promotion even. What does *that* mean?"

"Well in a good film, when someone is trying to hide something, they always butter up the person they don't want to talk. It's like a good magician doing sleight of hand. They want you to focus on the wrong hand and miss the actual trick. You might be getting buttered up."

"Really? You think? Hicks already went through the trial and nothing came of it. The smoke's cleared. Not sure what else he's hiding. Business is good at TB, and there's no need to butter me up."

Larry wagged a finger, "Don't get blinded by the sleight of hand. Which hand is the trick in? That's what we need to find out, Watson."

I stumbled back to bed needing a couple more hours of sleep. I had class and then work. I didn't want to close my eyes for fear of another Hicks nightmare. I did anyway, and nothing happened.

My dreams were free of nightmares. Besides, working at TB was becoming a nightmare of its own.

THE AIR on the pier turned from warm to cool, normal weather for Sea Lion Beach in November. Crowds thinned and yet TB hadn't seen this much business in late fall in her history.

I leaned against a support beam holding up the Ferris wheel and waited for Rodriguez to arrive. He would train me on the Wheel despite my hesitation of the promotion. I wanted to confront Rodriguez about his real name, whatever it might be, but I was a coward. The nightmares of Hicks and his behavior of late caused alarm.

A seagull sang out in the distance, and a gust of wind tossed up dust and trash on the pier. My attention averted down the pier toward a man holding a clipboard.

"Sorry I'm late. Had meeting with Hicks."

"Solve all the world's problems?"

"A TB problem. Kid working One Ball tipped off cusThomasers to which milk jug was easiest to knock over. Let's say he's probably looking for a job at Taco Bell," Kelvin said.

"Was it Santiago?"

"Mexican kid? Forgot his name already."

"How'd you catch him? Video?" I said with a smile.

Rodriguez looked up from his clipboard and clearly didn't like the joke, "None of your business. Let's get you trained so I can get out of here. I have more important things to do."

I nodded knowing my training would be brief and incomplete. But, that was par for the course of late. The family atmosphere and people-first mentality of TB had been decimated. In the past, guys like Santiago would've gotten a second chance. TB was not safe and getting worse each day.

Rodriguez sat in a chair behind the control booth of the Wheel and unlocked the case. "The green button on the far right is power. When you start your shift, make sure the key is turned clockwise. There's not much to it. Once you load the people in the cars, you hit this button," Kelvin said, pointing to a silver button on the left.

I nodded.

"How long do people ride?"

"Everything's auThomasated. Once people get loaded in their cars with lap bars fastened, you hit the button. The ride is timed for four minutes. You can never change settings from here. I have the power to change it."

"Never? What if a good looking girl is riding and I want a longer look?" I said slapping Rodriguez on the arm, who obviously was not my friend and had no intentions otherwise. He ignored the slap and slid out of the chair.

"Here's how you load people in the cars. Hold the car with the left hand and help people in with the right. Make sure it doesn't swing, and prop it with your foot. People will fall out. Trust me, it happens," he said, giving a threatening stare. I got a distinct "don't mess around on the Wheel" vibe.

"Is that what happened when the kids died?" I couldn't believe the words came out of my mouth. Didn't know what to do next except blurt out, "I meant in the loading area. People stumble out of the cars all the time."

Rodriguez closed the metal door on the car and with a hushed tone leaned into my face, "Careful with your words. You don't know what the hell you're talking about." I could smell his spearmint gum.

"I know more than you might think."

He jammed a finger in my chest and gave a smile, with a gold tooth emerging in place of his upper right canine, "I'll say it again. You know nothing. Never say it again. No one died on the Wheel."

"I have sources that tell me otherwise."

"You're a punk kid. What sources do you have?"

"Enough dirt on this place I could end it Thomasorrow... Spirit Child."

Rodriguez paused liked he'd seen a ghost and set the clipboard on the control booth. He pushed up his flannel sleeves like he wanted to fight, "What did you call me?"

"Did I pronounce it right? Not a common Hispanic name."

My mouth was getting me in trouble, and I didn't think about an exit plan. Was it too soon to go after these guys? Did I have solid evidence? I was just a college kid trying to make a few bucks and make sense of life for a summer.

"Who told you that?"

"What?"

"My real name."

"You admitting guilt?"

"Who told you..."

"I have sources."

"Tell me your sources now, ass hat."

I stepped back for fear Rodriguez would punch me in the face. "My sources are public," I said, pulling a wallet from my back pocket. I flipped it open a photocopy of a picture came into view. I held it at Rodriguez.

"That you in the photo? Funny thing. The name doesn't say Rodriguez. It says 'Spirit Child.' That's not a Hispanic name is it?"

Rodriguez glanced around the pier like a camera and audio device were recording our conversation. He whispered, "No. It's not. Name is Sioux. Where'd you get that photo?"

"You'd be surprised what you can find at the library," I said, showing Spirit Child a second photo. "This looks like Bill Hicks, if I'm not mistaken."

Spirit Child ripped the photo from my hand and gave it a look over, "Why's he wearing a headdress? He looks like an idiot."

"What do you mean? You know Hicks is obsessed with Native American culture, right? I caught him doing a Rain Dance in his office the other day."

Spirit Child looked puzzled and wouldn't let go of the picture. He took a second look, "I understand the Sioux obsession. You'd have to be blind not to notice. But, why'd the article talk about TB being on a Native burial ground?"

I scratched my head, "Wait, you're joking, right? You knew about Hicks buying property on a burial ground. Didn't he pay off a local Indian organization to keep them quiet? What do you know about Natives for California?"

"It's a local nonprofit that promotes Native American rights and educates people about our culture. I'm a member. That's where I met Hicks. Why?"

"I guess... I assumed Hicks paid off the organization. That's why he's pictured in the headdress. So, you know nothing about his association with this group?"

"Hicks came to weekly meetings. We'd discuss our heritage and what it's like to be Sioux and living in California. Talk about the latest right's violations. He said he was fascinated with the conversation and enjoyed the fellowship. Said it was like church for him. Took a liking to me."

"Liking how?"

"Hicks talked about his experience in the Dakotas, living on a Sioux reservation for a summer school project. He found out I was Sioux and wanted to know more. Didn't think much of it..."

"He didn't say anything about wanting to buy property on a Native burial ground? Never mentioned paying anyone off? Just a white Texan interested in Indians?" I asked, in an accusatory tone. I wasn't buying Spirit Child's story.

Spirit Child waited to collect his words and almost cried, but held back. "Hicks changed. He called me all the time, wanted to come over to my house and spend time with family. It got weird. He offered me a job at TB, a right-hand man type of job."

"Did he ever hurt you? Make threats?"

"Never, but he pays well and I do whatever he asks. My family struggles to survive, and this job has changed our lives. I don't want to mess it up."

The words of Spirit Child seemed genuine and off all in one. I was confident Hicks and Spirit Child were in cahoots and doing something shady behind the scenes. It seemed SC played the puppet to Hicks and would do whatever he asked, which included lying to my face. It was hard for me to reconcile SC not knowing about Hicks purchasing the property from the Native Americans. They were so close.

"You're telling me Hicks is safe? You never felt in danger, ever?"

"He says strange things from time to time. Like how he wants to take over the world and dominate the theme park industry. I see a driven businessman who wants to be the best. He's an old guy and wants to make a mark in his time left on earth. Any danger in that?"

I shrugged and leaned against the railing around the base of the Ferris wheel. My brain swam with confusion and questions. "Why does Hicks want me on the inside? He gives these promotions. What does that mean?"

"I don't know. He asks me to play the tough guy part, and I do. It's all an act. Tell no one," he said.

"You're shitting me, right? All the threats and tough stuff an act? That's hard to believe."

"Like I said, the pay is good. My family is stable. I'll do whatever Hicks asks. You being on the inside is part of Hicks' sickness."

"What sickness, like cancer?"

"No. Like insecurities. He wants young men he can control. I don't mind being controlled because of the cash. I told myself I'd get out the moment things got weird or illegal."

"He wants to control me?" I asked.

"Not in a creepy way. He wants people on the TB team who are loyal, *yes men*. It's all about Hicks. He wants TB to be the greatest show on earth. We are the ones to get him there."

"That makes sense, I guess. I won't worry about promotions if they are harmless."

"I wouldn't."

"Tell me this, why do you go by Rodriguez?"

SC laughed, "I use it because traditional names are not cool. Having a name like Spirit Child is not cool even for the Hippies in California. I also found ladies don't like dating the Sioux. It worked for Sherry. How's that going?"

"It's complicated. You hear she moved to the Midwest?"

"What? That doesn't make sense. I saw her mother the other day at the grocery store. Didn't talk to her, but know it was her. Sherry still lives at home."

"How long ago?"

"Two days ago."

"That's strange. She wrote me a note, telling me she was moving to the Midwest with the family. That was over a week ago and sounded like she was leaving soon."

"Maybe they haven't left yet?"

"Maybe. What else you know about Sherry?"

"I can tell you two things for certain. One, she was a great employee. She shouldn't have gotten fired. Two, it wasn't her fault those kids died. She had nothing to do with it. No one knows for certain what happened that day, but I was on the controls of the Wheel when a kid died."

"What do you mean?"

"Sherry went to the bathroom, and I took over the controls. The kids died when she was gone."

"I never got the entire story. Did a kid fall off the Wheel?"

Spirit Child shook his head no. "That's the strange part. I found a kid face down in the TB Tike area sand box. No one saw anything. The second kid was hunched over on a bench by the Sea Lion Flyer holding a corndog. Thought he died eating one of those nasty things, but cause of death was inconclusive."

"Why did Sherry get blamed when the deaths weren't her fault. No one died on the Ferris wheel."

Spirit Child said, "They needed a fall guy, or fall girl, in Sherry's case. She was an easy target."

"Didn't anyone see you working the ride when the kids died? Why didn't you get any heat?"

SC waved me to the platform of the Ferris wheel. He knelt down to the boards on the floor, unlocked a latch, and opened a door. SC pointed to the botThomas of a black hole, "I went down there. When all the attention averted to the dead kids, I made an escape."

"What's that, a secret tunnel?"

"Hicks had them put in a couple spots under the pier. He bored holes in the cement pillars that hold up the structure. They have stairs on the sides and exit doors at the botThomas. Don't know exactly why you need them, but it came in handy when I needed an escape plan."

"I'm guessing Sherry didn't respond kindly to your escape and what happened at the trial."

"Nope. Let's say that was the end of the relationship."

"Dirt bag move, don't you think?" I asked, wanting to punch the guy in the mouth. I wondered if Kelvin was the reason things never worked out for Sherry and I.

"Worst decision of my life. I liked Sherry."

"Well, glad things worked out for you," I said, rolling my eyes.

"Neil, please say nothing. These are not things I'm proud of or want people to know."

"Okay.. I guess." I didn't jump to any conclusions. Who could I believe these days?

I LIVED under no illusions that what might go down at TB was beyond my pay grade. With the help of Larry, Kelvin, and my research, I was confident the trails would make sense of the mess. Still, I needed bigger guns and more power.

That's when I called Uncle Thomas.

Dad's brother served the fine people of Oceanside thirty years as a detective. He moved around Oceanside PD and landed in Homicide. He retired ten years before the infamous summer of '79, but never left the game. Some say you never retire from police work. Retirement was forced upon you because of age. Many in law enforcement committed suicide after hanging it up, because they don't know how to deal with life after the force. Not Thomas.

Thomas Gordon a perfect member added to the team of wannabe detectives. I wanted to dig deeper into the world of Hicks and TB. I also didn't know what the hell I was working with. A college freshmen, working at a theme park and aspiring to write, was not sufficient for taking this situation where it needed to go.

Thomas arrived at the Roach Motel on a Tuesday night in November.

He walked through the door with little chitchat, despite us not seeing each other in five years. He tossed his coat and hat on the couch. I slid the folder of research across the dirty coffee table, piled high with film critic magazines, empty Styrofoam cups, and a full ashtray.

Thomas slumped into the itchy couch and twiddled his thumbs.

"Here's what we know. I've done a little legwork already. The articles and photos paint an ugly picture," I said, poorly trying to imitate *Kojak*.

Uncle Thomas twirled his Rollie Fingers mustache and opened the folder, "Impressive! Good work, kid. Could've used you while working in Oceanside. My department was filled with a bunch of morons. Reason I left the force."

He'd like to believe his own story. But Dad told me Thomas was asked to take early retirement. Too old school and didn't respect the new breed of officers and ways of doing things.

"Thanks, Uncle. Amazing what you can find at the public library. Look at the clippings and it'll give context to what we're dealing with at The Boardwalk."

He scanned one, picked up another, and held a third in better light. Thomas's thick rimmed glasses were not doing any favors. He tapped one photo, "Bill Hicks. I know this guy. We got an anonymous call on suspicion of domestic violence. Neighbor heard screaming. He lived up in the West Hills."

Like my dad, Thomas remembered the most mundane details. Maybe it's genetic.

"Is Hicks a violent dude?" I asked.

"Don't know. Nothing came of it. No charges filed,

although people in Oceanside thought something was off with Hicks. He came into town unannounced and ready to build The Boardwalk. No one knew where he came from. Small town people in Oceanside don't like surprises."

I hovered over the coffee table and pointed to one clipping, "See this guy. He's the right-hand man of Hicks. Strange thing. He didn't know anything about paying off Indians to buy the beach property to build TB. You think that's kosher?"

Thomas held the clipping almost touching his face and adjusted his glasses, "Listen to you, Kojak in the making. I like the way you think. One thing in detective work is true for all times: *trust no one*."

I nodded, "Kelvin sounded convincing. Hicks made no sign he paid off the Indians. He was sure of it."

"Who's that?"

"Spirit Child, he goes by Kelvin. It's a long story. He uses an alias at The Boardwalk because people don't take kindly to Indians."

"That sounds fishy. Indians in Oceanside are treated with upmost respect. At least from my perspective."

"No, he really used a different name. Said it helped with the girls." I said, pointing to the photo with his real Indian name.

"Regardless of his motivations. Anyone using an alias shouldn't be trusted. Huge red flags for me," he said, sifting through the rest of the articles.

"So, I shouldn't trust Spirit Child? You think he's blowing smoke? Not telling the truth?"

"Evidence doesn't lie. It's objective. Takes no sides, no loyalty to any party. The only loyalty is to truth."

I nodded again, "Any evidence we should consider from theses clippings? You're the pro."

Thomas smiled. "True. That's why I did my homework," Thomas said, opening a briefcase and opening a folder.

"Perks of being a detective is you meet resourceful people. IRS agent owed me a favor for helping him years ago. Wife was sleeping around and wanted me to find the guy."

"Tail on the side? I know that one well," I said shaking my head.

"Huh?"

"Never mind."

"Good time to cash in the favor," Thomas said, sliding an IRS tax document with Bill Hicks' name on top.

I scanned the page and could see it was a standard tax return, "You have Hicks' tax record?"

"Not that hard to get. You'd be surprised how clueless our government is," Thomas said while twirling his mustache.

"How does this help us?"

Thomas reached for a second, third, and fourth document, and shoved them in my direction. "I pulled the last ten years of tax records on Hicks. If he's doing anything financially uncouth, we'll see it."

I looked over the numbers and lost interest, "You find anything?"

Thomas stood and paced the room twirling his mustache, "Evidence is objective. Facts are objective. We are on a truth mission, and math doesn't lie. You can't manipulate what we see here. 2+2 is always 4."

"Okay, and..."

"Hicks gave hundreds of thousands of dollars to a local nonprofit called Natives for California."

"Yep, I know. Spirit Child told me Hicks supported the organization. So?"

"Hicks gave money to the organization in '75, '76, and every year since. This was right around the time he purchased land in Sea Lion Beach to build The Boardwalk. The tax record shows it all..."

"Okay, but what does this prove? Hicks could just be an overly enthusiastic Indian fan who likes supporting the organization. A wealthy guy who wants to write off tax deductions to charity, right?"

"How many overly enthusiastic white guys do you know supporting Native American organizations? The whites and Natives don't have the greatest relationship. Evidence is objective and doesn't care about our feelings. When you see smoke, there's fire."

"Is this enough for concern? What does it prove? Is it enough to prove Hicks is shady?"

Thomas nodded his head and gave a satisfying smile as he paced the room, "Kid, you're making a rookie mistake. Feelings are clouding your judgement. Let's not accept surface observations. We want truth."

"There's more under the surface? What?"

He gave out a shout, "Yes, there's more. I did a little digging on the Natives for California organization. I wanted to know if there's anything hiding behind the curtains. Know what I found? Mr. Spirit Child is a liar."

"Is the organization a front for the mob?"

Thomas frowned, "No. Not at all. It's a good nonprofit and doing good work. However, you said Spirit Child knew nothing about Hicks involvement in paying off Indians. Well..."

"Yes?" I asked, waiting in anticipation like a child with presents on Christmas.

"Spirit Boy was the bookkeeper."

"I know where this is headed."

"How in the hell a bookkeeper wouldn't see money flowing in and out from Hicks is beyond me."

"That dick hole. Totally lied."

"To add a cherry on the Sundae, Spirit Boy was on Hicks' payroll long before being hired at The Boardwalk. I checked."

"Shit. I fell for his bullshit and sad story. He told me how poor he was, how the job and money changed their lives."

"He might be a dirt bag, but he was poor. I checked his family's tax records too."

I smiled and laughed, "Really?"

"You gotta be thorough son."

I mirrored the pacing of Uncle Thomas and grasped my chin, thinking about all the connections. "So, Spirit Child is a liar. He had to know about the property, and Hicks paid off the Indian organization. Hicks and Spirit Child must be working together and doing something terrible trying to cover up the deaths of those kids. I think we're on to something."

Thomas nodded and closed the folder and placed it back into his briefcase, "I have a lot of time on my hands these days. Retirement makes for long days. I'd love to keep working on the case if you like. Pro bono," he offered.

"Please. I'm no detective and need all the help I can get. Don't know what to do next. Scared of opening this hornet's nest."

"Any other evidence you can share Kojak? What else I need to know?"

I snapped my fingers and remembered the conversation with Spirit Child, "He told me about a trap door on the

Ferris wheel. Hicks was under investigation and went to trial for the death of two kids. SC escaped through a trap door avoiding his name getting thrown into the trial."

"I know that case. Mistrial, not enough evidence."

"You know your stuff. Spirit Child told me there were hidden tunnels under the pier. He used one during the deaths of the kids. I don't know what it means, but can you check it out?"

"Where there's smoke, there's fire. I think no case ever has lack of evidence. You need to keep digging. I'll dig more."

I could tell the enthusiasm of Thomas was much higher than mine. I was at the end of my rope and didn't know what to think anymore. I thought about Sherry, and college was not that fulfilling. I worked a job with criminals, or at least we thought so. I wanted a summer redo, a fresh start. Kids weren't supposed to worry about these things, at least not yet.

"Thanks, Thomas. Let me know what you find."

He packed up his briefcase, put on a long, brown raincoat and top hat, and gave a nod disappearing into the beach air.

I knew what would cheer me up, a home cooked meal. My digestive tract couldn't handle another corndog from TB.

THE SCREEN DOOR of the house cracked, and I peered into the well-lit house. A short woman limped toward me. We almost collided in the foyer. She examined the street before closing it shut as if expecting a burglary. "Hey, baby," my mother said, kissing me on the cheek.

"You look skinny. Doing the speed-walking thing again?"

My mother grabbed onto the latest cultural movement and held tight for all of five minutes. Jogging with her friends equaled her attempt to ignore the mundane existence of housewife life in the suburbs of Oceanside.

She wiggled my chin, "Oh, no. I gave up speed-walking a long time ago. You need to come over more often."

It was true. I had spoken to mother a handful of times since the awkward divorce conversation months earlier. Avoidance was my weapon of choice. I guess I didn't want to deal with the inevitable. Dad still lived under the same roof, I had hoped things would work out. But that would change when the lawyers got their shit together. My folks held it together for my sister. She had one more year of high school. They tried to make senior year smooth as possible, at least that's what they told us.

I smelled pasta wafting from the back kitchen. "You hungry? I cooked your favorite," my mother said, with a small cough.

"You sure you're okay? Look a little pale."

Mom brushed her face with a frail hand, "I'm fine. Fighting a cold, that's all. When the weather changes it makes my allergies go crazy. Those Santa Ana winds, you know?"

I nodded and gave her a look over, not believing the allergy bit. We walked into the kitchen and looked across to see Kim working on homework. She lifted an eye and went back to work.

"Hey loser. How's algebra?" I asked.

"Shut it. I'd ask for help, but your grades senior year weren't the best. Everyone knows who the math genius in the family is, and it's not you."

She was right. Math never clicked with a brain wired for story. I needed subjects with room for shades of grey. Math and science were too exact.

"You talk now. But, wait for college level Calculus. It'll kick your ass. How'd your speech go in Perkins class?" I asked, licking sauce off a ladle swimming in a large black pot on the stove.

"I don't want to talk about it," Kim said, huffing and staring back into her work.

Kim was good at math. I was good at English and decent at public speaking. She'd rather die than give a presentation in front of her peers.

"Do you guys always have to fight? Everything 's not a competition, you know? Life is too short to fight," Mom said.

"You're right, Ma. Kim's so inconsiderate," I said, giving

her a small body squeeze. "You need to eat some pasta. You're skin and bone."

Mother ignored the comment and Kim chimed in, "Speaking of inconsiderate. I've seen little of you this summer. No visits? What's up with that Big Bro?"

I placed my hands in my jeans and stared at the yellow linoleum floor. I didn't have a good answer. "Good point Kim. I've called a couple times. But yes, I've been a little absent. No good excuses. Other than studying long hours, working hard at TB, and being a good neighbor in the community. And, I'm seeing a girl," I said.

"Is she real this time? Or another imaginary one?" Kim asked.

"Okay, the girl part isn't true. The other stuff is though. I'm getting good grades and working a lot."

"How's the new place?" Mom asked.

"The Roach Motel is great. It's a little dirty but works for two, working, single men. I like the beach views."

"Must be nice. I'm stuck here with the old people, and you're hanging out on the beach," Kim said, rolling her eyes.

"It's not like that. I'm so busy with school, work, and other drama. Don't have time to just hang out," I countered.

"Drama? Like who will buy the beer and cigarettes on Saturday night? Fighting over which movie to see at The Twin?"

"Kim... I'm appalled. Saying those kinds of things in front of mother. I'd never let those addictive narcotics near this body. It's a temple," I declared, rubbing my hands on my chest.

Kim stuck out a tongue and ignored the comment. Mother placed plates, silverware, and napkins on the kitchen table, "Let's eat," she said, and then stumbled.

I reached out, catching Mom before she hit the floor. "You okay?"

"I'm fine. Just a little dizzy. Fighting a cold, and a little dehydrated. Damn those allergies, like I said."

I stood her up and felt the bones poking through her sweatshirt. I dished the spaghetti, meatballs, and garlic bread onto the plate, then noticed one place setting missing. "Where's Dad? He eating with us?" I asked.

"No. He's eating in the study."

I didn't ask for an explanation. I heard this was routine after Dad got caught cheating.

"How are things on the home front? You guys figure anything out with the lawyers? Heard they're slow getting their stuff together."

Mom glanced at Kim and then back and me. I could tell Mom wanted to talk about something else. She sipped wine and twirled a piece of spaghetti on her plate, not eating it. "Things are on hold."

"What's on hold? Everything okay?"

She took a second sip of wine and stared up like trying to fight off tears before saying, "We're holding off on making the divorce official."

I lit up and took a swig of milk. "That's great to hear. You getting back together?"

"Not, exactly," Mom muttered.

I peeked at Kim and over to Mom. "What's going on?"

Kim wiped her mouth and then her eyes. I set my fork on the plate, "Can someone please tell me what the hell's going on?"

Mom sipped her wine and took a deep breath. "I have cancer."

I dropped my head feeling the heat from the spaghetti warm my face.

"Felt a lump. Went to the doctor, and they scanned me. Cancer," she announced, pointing to her left breast.

"What's prognosis? You'll be fine, right?"

She wiped her mouth, took a sip of wine, and placed her glass on the table. Then, she reached out a cold hand and placed it atop mine. "They think it spread. Not sure how much time I have. I know with everything going on this is heavy. We'll be fine... I promise, Neil... we'll be fine."

I glanced over to Kim who was staring at her plate of food and motionless, "You know about this?" I asked.

"I did, Bro, for a few weeks! You would've known too if you'd come around this summer," she said, tossing a napkin on the table and storming to her bedroom.

A guilt settled on me I've sensed for the last forty years. Hearing a mother had cancer was not good news for any child. But on top of that, I was absent that summer, looking out for myself and obsessing over a stupid job and a girl. I didn't call and was oblivious to her diagnosis. Larry died of cancer years later, and I never forgot that day. Maybe God was cursing me with the same disease because I was selfish. My problems at TB didn't seem all that big anymore.

I pushed back my chair, threw my napkin on the plate, and wrapped my arms around the neck of my mother. Her body felt small and frail, "Oh, Mom, I'm so sorry. I didn't mean to hide. I'd never moved out if I knew. Oh, God, I'm a terrible son..."

A convulsion of tears between the two of us didn't allow for audible words. My mother never held my absence against me until her last day on earth. She was full of grace and knew I was a kid trying to find an identity in a grownup world. I still feel the guilt.

"Don't cry Neil. I'll be fine. You didn't know. You're a

kid, and these are adult problems. I love you, Son," she said, kissing me on the cheek.

My sister wandered back into the kitchen and calmly sat back into her chair. She took a bite of food, "Sorry, Bro. I'm a little emotionally raw right now."

"Water under the bridge. You were right," I said.

We ate our food and said little for the next couple of minutes. My dad came into the kitchen and placed a dish in the sink, "Why all the sad faces?" Dad asked.

I spoke through a mouthful of food, "Mom told me."

"About what?"

"The cancer."

My dad nodded and I could see his eyes well up. I knew in that moment the love for Mom was still present and alive.

"Yeah, this is hard," he said, coming over and rubbing Mom's back.

"Why are you still getting divorced? Can't you make it work?" I asked.

"Let's not focus on that Neil. We want to kick this cancer's butt and worry about that later."

I nodded and wiped away another tear.

We all gathered in a circle and hugged like it was our last. The cancer would kick mom's butt, and it would only be nine months before it took her life. I don't remember exactly, but I think it was the last time we ever hugged like that as a family.

My parents never officially divorced.

I SEARCHED both sides of the pier, ensuring no one was watching. The only possible audience at 5 AM were homeless people and couples snuggled in a sleeping bag after a night of drinking. Neither were present.

Uncle Thomas had been working on The Boardwalk case the last couple of days and wanted to see the Ferris wheel. He thought the tunnels under the pier might be worth checking out.

I played with a small, silver padlock and glanced up at Thomas, "We need to get in and out. The cameras only operate during business hours," I told him while unlatching the lock and lifting the wooden trap door.

Heather assured me cameras and audio surveillance weren't on during off hours. My hunch was they were used for employees, and not customers. Hicks wanted his eyes on his team more than he cared about the outside world. I'd hoped Heather was right, or this might end badly.

Thomas peeked inside the hole and only saw a metal ladder and darkness. "You sure you want to go down there?" he asked, pointing and leaning to get a better look.

"Yes, sir. These tunnels might be the clue for unraveling the mystery surrounding TB. It may lead nowhere, but we need to cover all our bases."

"You're sounding more like a detective every day," he said.

I ignored the comment and trained a flashlight down the tunnel, then waved it side to side ensuring it was clear and safe to climb in. "Looks clear. You start down, and I'll close the door behind us."

Thomas stepped into the hole and secured his feet on the ladder. He glanced up at me, "This is a young man's game. I'm too old for this."

"You're young at heart," I said, slapping him on the back.

He shimmied down the ladder, wearing some kind of tight-fitting sweatpants and matching hoodie. His belly hung over the tight waist band.

I followed and stuck my head up out of the trap door. I gave a quick scan of the pier, looking for passersby. Finally, I shut the door and held the ladder with my free hand.

I yelled down to Thomas, "You, okay? Not sure where the ladder ends. I assume it'll bring us to the bottom of the pier column."

Thomas glanced up and covered his eyes, shielding his face from the flashlight and gave a thumbs up. "Careful where you aim that thing."

I heard the dripping of water and the echoes of ocean and wind from outside the cement cylinder. The ladder was rusting from years of sea water and air. Thomas's rubber soled shoes squeaked on the metal ladder as he descended. I stayed close. To be honest, the darkness in the cylinder freaked me out. Thomas was moving fast for an old guy.

"Slow down old man. This place is creepy," I said, flashing my light around the cylinder.

Thomas glanced up and gave another thumbs up, focused on the fifty-foot descent.

Soon, I heard the slap of Thomas's shoes hitting a cement bottom. "Neil, you will not believe this."

"What?" I called, my voice rattling against the hard surfaces of the pier column.

"I think we're below the beach. There's more real estate in these columns."

I reached the cement floor and expected to see an exit or door out to the beach under the pier. The column jetted to the right and opened into a high ceiling like you'd see in an underground sewer.

"Under the beach? How's that possible?" I asked.

"That's the only way this tunnel can keep going. Someone built this for a particular reason, probably not a good one."

Thomas's logic made sense, because I'd spent many years exploring the underside of the pier. It was no secret people generally used it for making out, smoking joints, or causing trouble. I didn't get into any of those things, especially the making out one. I walked the underside of the pier, reading novels and thinking about life. It was one of my favorite spots in Sea Lion Beach.

"It's like we're exploring the hidden city of Atlantis, except definitely not as cool, and way creepier."

I hit the side of the flashlight as the light flickered in and out. I aimed the light to the right wall and noticed the cleanliness. No graffiti or signs of use. Whoever built the tunnel didn't use it much, and few knew about it. I rubbed my hand along the wall and checked for dirt. It was like it had been power washed.

"You think it's weird this room is so clean? Like someone takes the time to clean it up, time to time."

"I was thinking the same thing. The only sign of wear is the corroded metal ladder. I wonder if the room was built later," Thomas said, scanning the room and kneeling to examine the floor.

I stepped further into the long corridor of the cement room, and Thomas was now following close behind. He examined the walls like looking at art in a museum.

The flashlight flickered again. I aimed it at the floor and gave it a hit. It flickered on and off, then back on as I noticed a door an inch from my nose. I gave a knock on the metal door, not sure what I expected to happen.

It was solid and made a deadened sound.

"A door," I informed Thomas, who was hunched over my shoulder.

"I see. Looks like a creepy door. Try the handle."

I peered down at the long, medieval looking handle and back at Thomas. He looked tense, like he didn't want it to open. I was confident the door wouldn't open. I brushed it with my hand and gave a gentle push down on the handle.

The handle flipped down, and the door yawned open and made a high pitched squeal.

Thomas waved me into the room with a nod. He looked hesitant.

I pushed the door into the room and flashed the light to the right wall. Then I noticed what looked like a blanket. I stepped further into the room and got a better look at the object.

It was not a blanket, rather, an animal skin. The skin spread wide across the wall and hung with purpose. Different symbols of lines, teepees, buffalo, bears, and a warrior Indian covered it.

I glanced back at Thomas who was now enjoying the creepy room. He caressed the skin and gave a smile. "It's soft. Someone hung this in here for a reason. They wanted us to find this stuff."

"Why?"

"I don't know. The door was open. If you're building hideouts in a tunnel and doing bad things, you don't leave a door unlocked. Just trying to follow the clues."

I directed the light to the left side of the room. A long wooden shaft with an Indian arrowhead dangled across another on the wall, and a mask with red and yellow lines on the face hung in the middle of the spears. I noticed a round circle of stones and wood sat in the middle of the room as I almost tripped on it. Residue lingered of a fire smoldering in the center.

I pointed to the mask with the flashlight, "Looks like someone is really into Indians. Sound like a guy we know?" I asked, giving Thomas a grin.

Thomas wiped the burned residue of wood with a hand and gave it a smell. "Someone was here within a few hours."

"We need to hurry up."

I turned to the back of the room and gave it a hit of light. A metal, twin-sized bed equipped with wool blankets rested in the corner of the space. I glided over and my heart sank. I'd hoped Hicks wasn't a pervert. Who knew?

Thomas lifted the blankets and asked me to shine the light on the sheets. They looked fairly clean and had no signs of abuse. He swept a hand across the sheets and lifted a hair.

He forced my hand with the flashlight on top of the hair and leaned in for a closer look. "Looks like a red one. You know anyone with red hair?"

I nodded. "Sherry Lewis. It's not Hicks or Spirit Child.

Bill's mostly bald with white hair. SC has jet black hair. Damn."

"Who's Sherry Lewis?"

"My girlfriend... ugh, no, kind of complicated. A friend. She was an employee involved in the lawsuit against The Boardwalk. I don't understand. She moved to the Midwest a few weeks ago."

"Don't assume the worst. We don't know if it's her hair. I'll keep it and see if we can find a match," Thomas said, dropping the hair in a plastic bag.

"How are we going to do that?"

"Do you have something she might've worn? Maybe a sample in your apartment?"

"I don't know. We weren't intimate or anything. Maybe in my car?"

"That's a good place to start."

I paused a couple beats and tried to erase Hicks doing something horrible to Sherry. "What's your take on a bed in a creepy room under a pier? I don't think it's for napping. Nothing to worry about, right?"

Thomas shook his head and gripped his double chin, "Whoever built this thing and left the fire burning, they wanted us to see it. The person left the door unlocked. The question becomes why?"

"You don't think someone hurt Sherry, do you?"

Thomas wrapped an arm around my shoulder and gave me a deep stare, "I've seen evil things in my day, stuff I can't repeat without reliving the hell. I also know, not all people are sick bastards. A good detective needs to find positive in all the evil. If not, you go crazy with assumptions. Let's get the facts. Find the evidence before we make conclusions."

I slammed a fist against the cement wall realizing it was a bad idea, "I hate Hicks. This has to be his little perverted

Indian lair. Who else would have a place like this under the pier? I don't know what the hell this guy is into, but he needs to stop. We will stop him."

Thomas yanked on a small bag, tied around his waist. He pulled out a Polaroid camera. "I'll take pictures. I want to see if any of these Indian artifacts will help in our case."

As Thomas snapped pictures, I wandered around the room feeling nausea in my stomach. I flashed the light on a wall we'd not explored. A second door similar to the front shown in the light.

I walked to the door and yanked on the handle. It didn't open.

Thomas finished taking pictures, and we made our way back out of the room. I pulled the door shut and said a prayer, asking God to protect Sherry wherever she might be. That might've been my first prayer.

We climbed the ladder. I opened the trap door and ensured no one was watching our escape. The pier was still clear as it only was 6 AM.

I hoped the cameras were not on at TB, or things might get interesting.

THE LIGHTS on the pier shut down as I locked a gate to the entrance of the Ferris wheel. Another day done. November crowds were small as the heatwave subsided. I stood next to the trapdoor and gave a look around, fearing exposure of what Thomas and I did earlier in the morning.

I turned the key in the control panel of the Ferris wheel and watched each row of lights disappear one by one. I removed the key, flipped down a metal cover, and gave a glance at a car swinging in the night breeze.

A hand touched my sleeve.

I flinched and yanked my arm away, like avoiding a bee sting. My heart raced as I scanned the darkened pier. No one.

The last voices of TB faded in the distance.

I scanned the left side of the Wheel where people entered the ride, then stood atop the trap door.

Thump. Thump. Thump.

What the hell?

Thump. Thump. Thump.

I knelt down and placed my ear over the door.

Thump. "Help me. I didn't do it. Help."

Thump.

I jumped back. Turned to the side and scanned the pier looking for people. I heard giggles of a couple at end of pier, in the distance.

"Kelvin, you here?"

No response.

Kelvin locked up the park and did a final walkthrough before leaving for the night. He worked late the entire time I worked at TB. I assumed he was messing with me.

Thump. Thump.

The sounds under the wooden door were getting louder and more violent. I hesitated and took a step back and waited to see if the sounds came back.

"Help us. We didn't do it. Help. Help."

A presence gripped my waist and spun me around and threw me to the ground. Its force fell on my back and pinned me to the ground. I screamed for help, my voice echoing into the void.

The presence held me to the ground for many seconds and released. It felt like an hour.

I jumped to my feet and dusted and glanced again to the Wheel cars overhead. Two, then three, and then four cars swung unprovoked.

"Who's doing this? What do you want?" I yelled into the cool, November air.

I felt a hand on my shoulder and spun around, putting up fists ready to fight.

"Who you talking to?" Kelvin said, holding his hand up in defense.

"Please tell me you saw that shit?"

"See what?"

"Did somebody put you up to this? Someone came

up behind me and threw me to the ground. Didn't you hear the voices, or see the cars swinging on the Wheel?"

Kelvin smirked and gave a small laugh looking at the clipboard and back at me. "You on drugs? Heather and Brock went home hours ago. There's no one here. I've been walking the grounds the last ten minutes. Not a soul around."

I rolled my eyes. "You're pulling my chain, right? How do you explain the voices?"

"Voices? There were a couple kids screaming down by Sea Lion Flyer. That's it..."

I grabbed his arm and pointed at the trap door. "Put your ear on the ground, and tell me what you hear."

Kelvin raised an eyebrow and obliged. "You need to get some rest kid. I think you're hearing voices in your head," he said, placing an ear over the trap door. "What am I listening for?"

"Voices. Little kid's voices yelling for help. 'Help. We didn't do it.'"

"Nothing. I only hear a voice saying, 'Neil needs help. He needs mental help,'" Kelvin teased.

I yanked Kelvin from the ground and stomped on the door, "I swear. Someone's messing around and playing games. I was grabbed and thrown to the ground and heard voices. Clear as day. I promise."

Kelvin raised his hands in innocence and snapped a piece of gum. "Easy, kid. No one's accusing you of anything. I believe you, seriously. Let's go home and sleep on it. Sound good?" he said, with a grin telling me he didn't believe a word I spoke.

"Speaking of sleeping. How did you sleep last night?"

"Excuse me?"

"Must be hard to sleep with a guilty conscious. I'm not stupid. I know you and Hicks are up to no good."

Kelvin tossed the clipboard on the control panel. I had his full attention. He stepped a few feet closer and craned his neck like he wanted to fight, "Like how, kid? Can you be more specific?" he urged, nose flared.

"Hicks paid off the Natives for California group. He paid them to keep quiet about the burial ground under the pier."

Kelvin turned his head a couple times, processing what I said and getting flustered, "How would you know? Who told you?"

"I know a guy."

"A punk kid like you knows a guy? I don't think so."

"You're a liar, Spirit Child. I know you've been on Hicks' payroll for longer than you led on. Don't play games. I know."

Kelvin slammed me down over the control panel and jammed a forearm in my neck. He turned red and foamed at the mouth and spat, "You don't know a damn thing about me. Who's telling you these lies?"

"Let's say I have family in the crime fighting business. He knows you were the bookkeeper for Natives for California. Am I right?"

Kelvin pressed harder on my throat, and it became hard to breathe. "You're right. But that doesn't mean shit."

"So... you're telling me a bookkeeper... wouldn't notice Hicks funneling large amounts of money into the company coffers? That seems convenient."

Kelvin calmed and spoke in a hushed tone, "I'll make you a deal. You keep your damn mouth shut, you live. And, you keep your job. If not, things get dark real fast."

I weighed the options and knew I needed Kelvin to stop

choking me, "I have enough to take you, Hicks, and TB down in a phone call. No more TB... no more cash."

I needed to breathe.

Kelvin released my neck and took a step back from the control panels on the Wheel. He wiped his mouth where a foam of spit had accumulated, "I was desperate. I needed help. My family needed help. It was an easy solution, and Hicks made it happen."

I caressed my swollen neck, "I don't give a shit. You lied. I trusted you and thought you were a decent guy."

"Not everything was a lie. My family's poor and Hicks gave us a shot out of poverty. All true."

"You knew about the property? The burial ground?"

Rodriguez nodded. "I was the bookkeeper, after all. And yes, Hicks put me on the payroll before TB."

"What for?"

"Kind of fuzzy. He loved Sioux culture and felt bad destroying the burial ground. I think making me a personal assistant eased his conscious. I needed the money and didn't ask questions. But beyond that, I don't see Hicks as a bad dude."

I tapped my toe on the wooden deck and gave a half smile, "How am I going to believe you? Cameras. Audio surveillance. Paying off organizations to keep their mouths shut. Rigged trials. You're in bed with the enemy. Hard to believe Hicks is a straight shooter."

Kelvin sighed, "Things look bad, I know. He wanted everyone to win with the purchase of this property. I could've reconsidered, but I didn't think his intentions were malicious. Hicks isn't evil. He pays his taxes, is involved in the Oceanside community, and shoots straight. Weird, yes, but still a straight shooter."

I wanted to believe Kelvin. I did. The look in his eyes seemed genuine, but I had seen it before.

A wad of keys sat propped on the control panel. I pushed Kelvin aside and leaned down to the trap door. Unlocked the padlock and propped it open.

I leaned over the hole and stared down into the black abyss, "You know what's in there?"

Kelvin smirked, "I told you about it. Pier columns have ladders and exit doors. Tunnels of escape."

I scratched my head in confusion. Kelvin seemed nonchalant about what Thomas and I saw. "You know *everything* that's down there?"

"Yes, I told you."

"How about the Indian artifacts, bed, and locked rooms?"

"What do you mean?"

"You don't know about the locked room and bed under the pier?"

Kelvin crossed his arms, and his eyes told me he was confused.

"My uncle and I went under the pier. We found creepy shit in the tunnel. There's a room, and it didn't look normal."

"No, man. I've only been in the tunnel and out the exit door. I know nothing about a creepy room and bed. Sounds perverted…"

"That's what I thought. You think Hicks is involved?"

"Probably. He knows every corner of TB. If he doesn't do it, it doesn't get done. He must've put that room in after the deaths of those kids. That was the last time I was down in the tunnel."

Kelvin and I stood over the hole and shook our heads. He needed to see for himself.

THE NEXT MORNING, I met Spirit Child near the Ferris wheel and replayed the tunnel adventure. He rubbed his blurry eyes and took a sip of coffee.

"It's too early bro," he said, adjusting a wool cap and yanking on his sagging black sweatpants.

"Don't want the cameras to see us. We need to get in and get out," I said.

"How'd you know about the cameras?"

"I have sources. Heard they operate only during business hours. 5 AM is not prime time for corndogs and the Sea Lion Flyer," I said.

"Someone's giving away all our secrets. You said the tunnel's not an exit out to the beach. Tribal stuff, bed, and other creepy things? I need to see this."

I nodded and unlatched the padlock giving a shot of light down in the tunnel. "Stay to the right and follow the ladder down. When you get to the bottom, you'll see a cement pad. Hang a right and it'll lead down a corridor to a metal door. That's where the creepy shit is."

Spirit Child turned on his flashlight and gave me a thumbs up.

I climbed down the ladder, and he shut the trapdoor behind us. Darkness enveloped the tunnel. SC followed behind, waving his light and exploring the surroundings.

"I remember this. Been awhile, but I recall the rusty ladder."

I gazed at the ladder, standing on the cement pad at the bottom. Spirit Child dropped with a thud. "You notice how clean the walls are?" I asked, wiping a hand over the cement.

SC touched the wall behind me. He shined a light to the left and pointed at a metal door, "You see that door? Goes right out to the beach. It empties under the pier. I used it last time I was down here."

I trained a light to a door on the right, "Come and follow me. This is the part you missed."

We meandered down the cement corridor until we stopped at the first door. I slapped the door and smiled at SC. "You thought tunnel was a simple exit to the beach? Think again."

Spirit Child took a step back and examined the door like a contractor looking for squareness. He slid his glove covered hands across the seam. "The door's new. And, the cement opening around the door is new. It smells like fresh cement."

I flashed my light at the top and bottom of the door and pretended I could tell the difference between a new and old door. "Okay. What does that mean?"

"I missed the door because it didn't exist. This room wasn't here last year. The door's new. The cement's new. This is a new area, that's what I think."

"Does that explain why the walls are so clean?"

"Most likely."

I gripped the handle of the door and gave a firm push toward the ground. "Let's see the money room."

The door squeaked open, and we both shined light into the room. Everything was the same from the day before. Bed, Indian artifacts, and animal skin hanging on the wall.

Spirit Child strolled through the room like he was walking the halls of the Natural History Museum in Los Angeles. He brushed the animal skin and leaned in to examine the symbols painted on the surface.

"Symbols are Sioux. That's my tribe."

He strolled to the other side of the room and tapped the tip of a spear hanging on the wall. SC rubbed the surface of the mask that hung in the middle of the spears. "Arrowheads made of quartz. A common material, but one the Sioux would use. The mask is an authentic Sioux Chief replica. All authentic Sioux stuff."

I gave a nod toward the metal bed and flashed a light on it. The pillow, sheets, and blankets were neatly made and undisturbed. "Thoughts on the bed?"

A voice from behind echoed in the room. We turned around, with hearts racing.

"That's the question of the day. What kind of person has a bed in a creepy tunnel like this one?"

Uncle Thomas flashed a light in my face and I covered my eyes from being blinded.

"Dammit, Thomas. You scared the shit out of us. What are you doing here? I hope no one saw you. I don't want anyone getting suspicious."

"Doing detective work for thirty years gave me insomnia. When I was on the squad, I lost a lot of sleep running every case in my head through the night. My wife hated sharing a bed with me, because

I'd wake up in the night and go to the study to work on evidence. I had one of those last night. Ever since we came in here, I needed to know more. There's something here that unlocks the mystery of Hicks and TB."

Spirit Child asked, "Who's this guy?"

"Oh, yeah. Uncle Thomas, this is Spirit Child. My uncle is a retired detective and helping me out."

"You hired a detective? Is he spying on me? The Boardwalk?"

"No it's not like that. When I found out about the tunnel, he wanted to see it. Thomas is a good guy."

"Why should I trust him?"

"If you're innocent there's nothing to worry about, right?" Thomas asked.

"I haven't done nothing wrong. Don't need no detectives watching me, though. I need this job, you hear?"

"You sound a little defensive. Sometimes a sign of guilt. Not always. It seems odd you'd be so close to a crook like Hicks and not know anything about his personal life. Aren't you his assistant?"

Spirit Child looked at me with sad eyes and back at Thomas, "I told Neil everything. Yes, I was the bookkeeper at Natives for California. I got on Hick's payroll. I don't know about anything else."

Thomas's hands were on his hips and his face said he wasn't convinced with SC's plea. He reached into a pack on his backside and opened a small plastic bag. He held a hair in the flashlight. "You might be naïve to the dealings of Hicks, but we found this hair on the bed over in the corner. That doesn't look like man hair. It smells like woman's shampoo. You want to guess what that means?"

SC shook his head and stared at the floor. He looked up.

"Is Hicks a bad man? Did he do bad things? I swear I don't know about any of this, whatever *this* is."

"That's why we're here. Evidence doesn't lie. It can't," Thomas said, with conviction.

Spirit Child held up hands in surrender and pleaded with Thomas. "I don't know what this room's all about. It wasn't here a few months ago. I sure as hell don't know what a bed is doing down here with a woman's hair on it. I don't want to know, really. But I swear guys, this has nothing to do with me. I can't speak for Hicks."

"A good detective would never accuse you of anything. First, why would an Indian kid have artifacts hanging on the wall of a creepy tunnel under a pier? I know you love your heritage. It's just cliché to hang Indian stuff in the residence of a real Indian, or a creepy tunnel. Second, we all know Hicks is obsessed with Indian culture. It would make all the sense in the world to have something like this for him to visit. We still don't know why and what his purposes are. On the surface it doesn't look good."

Spirit Child nodded and agreed with Thomas. "I don't like dark rooms. Hate going to the garage at night if I can avoid it. This place gives me the creeps."

"So Mr. Spirit Child, what reasons would Hicks build a space like this cozy tunnel?" Thomas asked.

Spirit Child leaned against one wall and rubbed his chin a couple times. "I know he loves Sioux culture, but he doesn't keep it a secret. I've caught him doing a Rain Dance in his office. My only thought is he's doing something he shouldn't be. This doesn't seem like a place to just hang out with friends and family."

"I've seen the dance too," I said. "It doesn't seem right. I don't know what Hicks is trying to say with this room? What's he doing in here?"

"Would any other employees know about the tunnels?" probed Thomas.

"Nope. I'm the only one with a key... but others know where to access them," Spirit Child said and glared at me.

Thomas and Spirit Child continued to put their heads together and see what motive Hicks might have. Why have these rooms? I walked over to another door in the back corner. It was one I noticed the other day.

Locked.

"Hey guys. Can anyone get this door open?"

Uncle Thomas flashed his light to the corner with the door and reached in his backpack. He fiddled with the pack and found a small wire. He stuck it into the lock and jiggled a couple times. The locked popped, and the door yawned open.

We all flashed our lights into a second room.

THE ROOM WAS EMPTY, a solid cement box with no beds, Indian artifacts, or skins hanging on the walls. Bigger and longer than the first room. I flashed my light in the corners of the space to see if worth exploring.

I trained the flashlight on the ground and followed the path of light. A rise in the middle of the floor caught my attention. Thomas and Spirit Child followed in behind.

I knelt down and noticed the floor of the second room wasn't cement. It was dirt mixed with patches of moss.

With light reflecting in the eyes of the others, I waved them over. They knelt in close. "Floor isn't cement. It's dirt and moss. Rest of the tunnel is cement. This is the only natural element we've seen," I said, swiping a hand across the floor and examining it with light.

I flashed the light further into the room and discovered the mound continued its incline toward the cement ceiling, like someone buried a VW Bug in the middle of the room.

I climbed the gentle incline and glanced back at the guys. "Look at me, up here. Whoever built the tunnel worked around the mound. What do you think?" I asked.

Spirit Child climbed the incline and bent down on the ground. He swiped the ground to examine the materials. "Looks like a small Indian burial mound."

"Did you say burial mound? Did you mean 'ground?'"

"More accurate to call them 'mounds.' Indian burial mounds are all over the country. But, I'm sure this isn't one."

"Why not?"

"Can't say for certain, but it is odd to see an Indian burial mound near a beach. Maybe it's dirt they didn't want to level before cementing in the tunnel. Workers got lazy."

I snapped my fingers and glanced at Thomas who was playing with the dirt on the mound. "Hicks bought the property for The Boardwalk, knowing it was an Indian burial ground... mound. That article, it had the story about the Natives killing the Europeans and vice versa, right?" I said, trying to recall the research I'd done at the library.

Thomas nodded. "Yes sir. I remember the story. Yet how can we verify this is the site? Spirit Child doesn't think it's an Indian burial mound."

I flashed my light further up the mound. "Evidence never lies, right? It can't. We'd need to see evidence of bone..."

"Bones?" Thomas said, holding up a slender, white object, that looked like an arm bone. He waved us to the back side of the mound.

A pile of bones and skulls formed a perfect circle at the back side of the mound. A small batch of dirt formed a smaller mound next to the circular graveyard.

"Holy shit. There's your answer SC," I said.

SC leaned over the circular bone structure and picked up a skull. "These bones are unearthed. They would never be laid this perfect and in this shape if legitimate. Many times, an Indian burial mound would have coffins underneath the hill. A person would have to dig them up and remove the bones from the coffin. Whoever did this spent a lot of time digging."

"This is Hicks, right? What sick person would take the time to dig up an Indian grave? Only a dude obsessed with Natives, like Hicks," I said.

A voice echoed through the cement room.

"That's right. Only a sick old man obsessed with Indians would dig up hundred-year-old bones. I don't regret it one bit. These are my people."

We turned to see Hicks standing at the doorway holding a flashlight, dressed in headdress, and wearing an animal skin. His face was painted blue and yellow, striped like the mask in the other room.

Spirit Child glanced at Hicks and gave a wide smile. "You're kidding, right? I think that's a little too far. Besides, you're not a real Sioux."

Hicks grinned and scanned who was in the room. "I beg to differ, partner. In college, when I lived on the reservation, we made it official."

SC raised an eyebrow and laughed, "How's that? A tribe and their tribal Chief determine who's a true member. How would a white man from Texas be accepted by the Sioux?"

"It's the luck of the Irish, only I'm not Irish. Turns out my deadbeat dad was part Sioux."

"I find that hard to believe. White men from Texas having Sioux in their blood is like winning the lottery. Rare, unless there's intermarriage in the family."

"Don't know who, but someone in my lineage married a Native. The tribal Chief determined it sufficed. Welcomed into the Sioux family. So, looks like we're family... Spirit Child."

"Sounds like bullshit."

"Why do you want to hurt me? We're family. That's why I put you on the payroll. I wanted to run a family business. That's what a loyal family does."

Spirit Child smirked, "You only care about money. I don't think family is your primary motivation. The Boardwalk Way is a bunch of lies and shit. You took this land from the Natives for your own gain, like every other white man in history. Your words are just a pile of dirt," he said, pointing to the mound behind him.

"Oh, son. All I wanted was for us to be family. I never had children of my own. Well, at least ones I liked. You were to be my Native son."

SC shook his head and kicked up dirt.

Hicks' countenance went from tender to a terrifying look of anger. His painted face scrunched and headdress cocked to the side, "Damn you. I gave you and that wretched family of yours all kinds of money. If I'm greedy, you're no different. You didn't complain when I wrote you a check every week. The least you can do is be grateful."

SC moved down the mound and pointed a finger at Hicks, "Hey, don't manipulate me. You know what you were doing with the land deal. You don't give a shit about me, my family, or my people. The success of The Boardwalk is all you care about. That's your family. The Natives were getting in the way. So you paid them, and me, and my family to keep quiet. I'm guessing you paid others to keep quiet in the trial, too."

Hicks nodded. "You're a smart kid. Got it all figured out. Makes me proud. But, sometimes people aren't loyal. Think the world revolves around them. Don't care what happens to others. They open their big mouths and hurt people."

"Like who?" I asked.

Hicks turned toward the entrance and gave a nod to someone hiding in the dark. A man dressed in Indian garb came into the room pushing a hand cart. A woman laid on the cart dressed in Indian attire. Her face covered in blood and cuts.

Hicks slapped the side of the hand cart, "Like this bitch. She was on the payroll too. Didn't grasp the Boardwalk Way. She decided loyalty wasn't for her. Opened her big mouth and had to pay for her transgressions."

Sherry Lewis laid against the cart whimpering, her mouth muzzled with rope and duct tape.

"If I'm not mistaken, I think two of you were shacking up with this whore."

I stepped toward Hicks to punch him. He pulled a spear from his side and waved it in my direction as if to say "don't think about it." I stepped back.

"Did the whore comment make you mad Neil? I'm sorry, but she is. I don't know who else she slept with at TB. But it's a high number."

"You don't need to talk like that," Thomas piped in.

"Oh, hello Detective. Did a little background check on you. Thanks for coming in the middle of the night to my lair. The video cameras thank you."

Thomas shrugged his shoulders and mouthed "I'm sorry."

"You're all a bunch of morons. I'll be happy when you're gone from the earth. Kind of like the kids buried underground. Those kids killed by the Sioux. I heard the Europeans did the same. An eye for an eye, I guess," Hicks chuckled with a twisted grin.

Sherry whimpered and made noises like a puppy needing food.

"What are you gonna do? You don't think we can hold our own? I'm not scared of you or your friend," I said.

As I spoke the words, Thomas emerged from behind me and Spirit Child. He held a pistol toward Hicks and the Indian. "In the background check, you must've caught I served Oceanside for thirty years as a cop. That means I know how to use this thing," Thomas asserted, raising his gun.

Hicks smiled and raised his hands in the air. "I don't need guns to fight this battle. I have a higher source of power. The Spirits of the Natives," Hicks said, then yelped and hollered.

He raised his hands and acted like he was lifting the ground. He prayed, "Grandfather Great Spirit. All over the world the faces of living ones are alike. With tenderness they have come up out of the ground. Look upon your children that they may face the winds. And walk the good road to the Day of Quiet. Grandfather Great Spirit. Fill us with the Light. Give us the strength to understand, and the eyes to see. Teach us to walk the soft Earth as relatives to all that live."

The room felt heavy with a presence you could cut with a knife. My stomach ached and the other guys fell over. Thomas dropped the gun on the ground and grabbed his chest.

I glanced at the ceiling. Small figures swirled and dive-bombed through the room. They were children dressed in clothes from another era. Hicks continued to pray and yell and holler out incoherent words.

"What is this? Stop it. Please," I cried, leaning over on my knees and covering my head.

"This is for all the ways your people have harmed the Natives. Our families didn't deserve to be treated like this in

America," Hicks called. His eyes closed and he raised his hands high.

"Stop. You're not even an Indian. You're a business man from Texas. The Sioux are not your people," I said.

"These children are family," Hicks declared, smiling as the spirits swooped around the room.

Thomas kneeled on the floor and looked for his gun. He grabbed the gun and attempted to climb to his knees. The children flew up and down and around his head, screaming at this point. A light splashed against the walls and our faces.

He held the gun toward Hicks with a wobbling hand. "You're a sick man, Hicks. This ends now."

Before Thomas could pull the trigger the Indian standing next to Sherry charged him with a spear. The spear hit the hand holding the gun and slipped up to his face puncturing the side of his neck.

Uncle Thomas dropped to his knees with eyes wide open and keeled over, rolling down the side of the Indian mound.

"Looks like we have another body for the grave," Hicks said, fiddling his fingers and acting calm about what happened.

"Anybody else want to be a hero today?" Hicks said, with a grin.

I glanced over to Spirit Child who was on all fours and holding his hands over his ears. "What's that noise? Make it stop," he shouted through the commotion of the room.

A high pitched squeal, sounding almost like a baby crying, now filled the room. "Hear it? That is the sound of suffering and injustice," Hicks said, raising his hands toward the ceiling.

WE LAID near the floor of the room and didn't know how to stop the spirits. Hicks kept praying, yelling, and hollering out incoherent chants. I peeked toward the entrance. Lights and figures entered into the area.

A man wearing a black uniform jogged into the room with gun drawn on the Indian and Hicks. A second man came in behind them.

"Freeze! Hands up!"

It was the Oceanside PD. A police officer jammed a gun into the back of Hicks and he dropped his spear. The second officer did the same, and the Indian dropped his spear. Both men were wrestled to the ground and placed in restraints.

"You have the right to remain silent," the officer recited and gave the rest of the standard police spiel.

The moment Hicks lowered his hands and stopped chanting the spirits ceased. The room was silent, and the heavy presence subsided.

I ran to the other side of the mound and found Thomas in a puddle of blood. I laid a hand on him and said a prayer under my breath. Didn't know if I should pray to God, or gods, or Indian spirits. It didn't matter, whoever was listening would do.

Thomas moved to his side and moaned. I waved down a paramedic who just arrived in the tunnel. Two men knelt next to my uncle and assessed his neck wound. He had lost a considerable amount of blood, but it sounded like he would be ok.

The police officers took away the Indian and Hicks and worked on Sherry. She had a distant look in her eye. They removed the gag and tended her wounds. Oddly, she seemed happy to see me.

I stood next to the officer who was pulling the tape from her mouth and untying her hands from the back of the cart.

"You couldn't get rid of me this easy," I said, realizing I hadn't seen Sherry's red hair in some time.

She fluttered her eyes.

I didn't know where to start. "So, yeah. I got the letter. I assume you never made it to the Midwest."

"Plans got derailed. I didn't want to move. It was Hicks' idea. Well, more precisely, he was planning on kidnapping me, as you can see," she replied while holding up her wrists covered in rope.

I scratched my head and tapped the handle off the metal hand cart. "You never were moving to the Midwest with your family? The letter was a lie?"

"All Hicks' idea. I would've called you. Unfortunately, Hicks ruined my plans. He told me I wasn't loyal, and I'd have to pay for my actions. Well... it's all over now at least."

Standing back, I looked Sherry over. I couldn't believe how easy going she was over the turn of events. Sheepishly the question came out, "Did he hurt you? I mean..."

Sherry released herself from the cart, and an officer

helped her to the ground. "No, that old man's all talk. The cuts and blood are fake. Hicks thought it would make it more dramatic." She wiped red paint from her cheek with the back of her hand.

"Wait. You're telling me Hicks staged this entire thing?"

"Not, exactly. After two days of being kidnapped at his house, he didn't know what to do with me. He thought I was withholding information, that I had led you to the evidence you found and questioned Kelvin over. He assumed I squealed about the payoff in the trial and more. But I already told him everything I knew. I didn't kill those kids. We don't know what happened that day. It's a mystery."

I laughed and shook my head. "What a moron."

"I got a question for you, Neil. Where did the cops come from? You guys were screwed if they didn't show."

A skinny blonde haired kid ran over to us with a giant smile. "Neil, you okay? I did what you told me."

"My buddy Brock is the hero. I got nervous about the cameras. I told him to call the cops if anyone followed us, just in case Hicks tried to pull anything while we were in the tunnel. Brock told the cops a homeless guy was shitting on the pier."

Brock glanced at Sherry and smiled. "How are you doing? I haven't seen you in a while."

"It's a long story."

I turned to check on Spirit Child, who finally passed the medic inspection. I gave him a hand slap and side hug, "You okay? That was crazy, right?"

SC shook his head, and a tear formed on his eyelid. "Man, Hicks was messed up. I didn't know the extent of the spiritual stuff. He *really* wanted to be Sioux, didn't he?"

"I'd say so."

"Neil, I'm sorry, man. Probably not what you signed up for."

"Nope. I wanted to make a little cash for gas and college, that's all. I didn't need all the extra drama."

"We cool? I'm sorry for being an ass most of the summer. Remember, all an act," he said.

"No worries. Just let me ask you a question. You remember that day you warned me about TB and Sherry. You said, 'be careful.' What was that about? You denied it before."

"You said that before. I have to plead the 5th, since I don't remember ever saying those words. I'm not even sure what kind of car you drive."

"Really? No recollection?"

"None. Probably thought it was me. I'm not the only dark haired Indian in Oceanside," SC smiled.

SC put a hand up to pause me for a moment and walked to Sherry, "We cool? I know things didn't end great. You know by now, I'm Sioux and not Hispanic. That was lame. I need to embrace who I am. I don't need to be ashamed of my roots, even if it got us all in a sticky situation."

Sherry smiled and didn't seem to care about it anymore. "I'm good. I'm just glad we're all safe and we can put the summer of '79 behind us."

We all nodded in agreement.

It hit me I'd need to find a new job. College and gas would not pay for themselves. I assumed Hicks would go to jail for a long time, and The Boardwalk would not make it through the next year. Regardless, I think a new job was in order.

I climbed up the ladder in the tunnel and let the cops

and paramedics do their work. It was late morning and people moved around the pier.

I placed my hands in my pocket and enjoyed a minute of quiet in the cool morning at Sea Lion Beach. I stood at the base of the Ferris wheel and smiled.

A hand touched my shoulder as I stared at a car on the Wheel swaying in the breeze. This time the presence wasn't heavy. It was light and comforting, like a friend telling me everything would be okay.

The summer of '79 was forever etched in my mind as crazy and mysterious. Still, maybe it's the mystery of life that makes it worth living.

You KNOW that job at the school newspaper I wanted? Well, I got it, and didn't need to worry about college and gas after TB. It wasn't a lot of money, but it paid the bills. I lived with Larry for most of college until something crazy happened.

I got married.

I wasn't totally honest about Sherry. Yes, she was confusing, and I never knew where I stood most of '79. But, I guess the intense experience with Hicks and the stuff at The Boardwalk brought us together. She finally said "yes" to a date. And, we went on The Ferris wheel before it closed in '80.

We married after college. I think about her almost every other day. She was the love of my life and always will be. She died five years into our young marriage. Car accident.

Never had children, but we enjoyed an amazing five years of love. I think Sherry caused my other two marriages to fail. Never recovered from the love of '79. Sherry was the benchmark, and that wasn't fair to my other two wives. At least, that's what my therapist thinks.

Whenever I see an amusement park, theme park, or Ferris wheel, I remember the days at the Boardwalk. Strangely, Sherry and I never discussed the children's spirits from the tunnel incident. Maybe we never wanted to believe it happened, too bizarre to wrap our brains around. Maybe it was a secret that needed to be ours until we met with the spirits. Who knows? But, it meant a lot to me during a difficult summer.

The hand on my shoulder is what I believe helped me fight cancer. A presence that never left during good and painful times. I'm not a religious man, but that presence has saved me many times over, and I consider it my guardian angel.

My therapist thinks I'm crazy and kids the same. But, someone is watching over me, like they were at The Boardwalk.

Those kids that died in '79 are still a mystery. No evidence. No eye witnesses. I don't know if the spirit-children seeking justice after hundreds of years. Maybe because Hicks bought the property on an Indian burial ground... or is it mound?

I don't know what it means. But, everything happens for a reason. I'm glad to be alive. My therapist told me to tell my story, to share a significant event in my life. The summer of '79 is one of those. I tried to tell it the best I could remember.

Hope you enjoyed it. Remember, be safe, and be careful on the Ferris wheel. You never know who might be watching you.

Neil Gordon,

. . .

July 1, 2016

The Boardwalk was inspired from colliding forces. First, a crazy event called NANOWRIMO (National Novel Writing Month), where hundreds of thousands of people compete to write a first draft of a novel in 30 days (50,000 words).

I've competed in the event for the last four years and loved every minute. It cultivates an environment of fun and challenge trying to get those words on paper before the clock ticks midnight on November 30.

So, as I was thinking about the event, I needed an idea. I had just read Stephen King's *Joyland* and loved the idea of haunted amusement parks. This was the second influence. The novel was a departure from King's typical dark horror, but was a beautiful mystery and coming of age story that's great.

I grew up in the backyard of *Disneyland* and *Knott's Berry Farm* in California. Despite living by the beach we had nothing like a *Coney Island* or a theme park on the beach. I wanted to create a world where this was possible.

That's why the Boardwalk is a fictional small theme park where kids could hang out. Maybe because I didn't have it as a kid, I needed it now.

Third, I wanted a mystery element behind the story. Wasn't sure what that might be or how it would work. I ran across an article about a haunted amusement park on the East Coast in the 60's. A wealthy man bought the park and learned it was on an Indian burial ground. That was a freaky idea, I thought.

I wanted to bring in the mystery element and tie it to Native American culture. That's why we have Bill Hicks and his obsession with the Sioux people. You get Spirit Child, who's not Hispanic, by the way. I didn't want to make that the entire book but hope the elements work.

Fourth influence. I was born in 1979 and thought it would be the timeline for the book. It was fun trying to bring in pop culture elements from this era.

Last, the coming of age element. I love coming of age stories like *The Body* from King and movies like *The Goonies*. We all have these experiences that shape and form life. Neil Gordon is looking back on his life because he's got The Cancer. I think sometimes we don't realize how good and bad things shape the trajectory of life.

The Boardwalk was so fun to write. I love Neil, Sherry, Kelvin, Bill Hicks, Brock, Gordie Gordon, Larry, and Kim. I think in a strange way we can all relate to these people. We know crazy people are into crazy things, and we all have crazy families.

I hope the book makes you think about love, longing, and what matters in life.

But, be careful on the Ferris wheel!

Thanks for reading...
   November 2016
   Ryan J. Pelton

ENJOY THIS BOOK? YOU CAN MAKE A BIG DIFFERENCE!

If you loved this book, you can help me reach more readers with a few easy steps:

(1) REVIEW THIS BOOK

Reviews are one of the best helps for getting these stories out to the world. My publisher doesn't have the financial muscle of New York, but does have an even more potent weapon. A bunch of loyal and committed readers. By leaving an honest review other readers can find and take chances on my books. Just go to the site you purchased this book, search for the title, and leave a review. Much thanks in advance!

(2) SUBSCRIBE TO MY EMAIL LIST

Building a relationship with my readers is the greatest joy of my writing life. I'm not just a writer, and love sharing things I'm learning, reading, and pondering. If you want an occasional update on the latest Dexter O'Kane novels, and my other writing projects. If you'd like to hear about things in my world, get some interesting links, and book updates please do so below. I also give special deals and other cool insider goodies to my VIP List. Sign up today, and join the fun! RyanJPelton.com

(3) TELL YOUR FRIENDS

Word of mouth is still the best marketing there is, so I would love if you gave a shout out to your family and friends about this book, and the others I have written. You can find a comprehensive list of my fiction books at: ryanjpelton.-com/common-grace-publishing.

Thanks again for your help, and thanks for reading!

ABOUT RYAN J. PELTON

Ryan J. Pelton is a pastor by day and a writer by night. He often warns his church if they mess with him, they'll end up in his books. Ryan is best known for his mystery/thriller novels for adults and children. He also writes

nonfiction, on a variety of subjects from a Christian perspective. Ryan enjoys music before the 90s, naps, tacos, and reading, as all right-thinking people do. When not writing, you can find Ryan with his family in Kansas City, Missouri, rooting for the Chiefs, Clippers, and wishing the ocean was closer. Join the fun at Ryan's online home: ryanjpelton.com.

ALSO BY RYAN J. PELTON

Dexter O'Kane

Hired Gun

Stranger Danger

Color Blind

First Blood

L.A. Dreams

Dexter O'Kane Box Set (Books 1-4)

Stand Alone Novels/Novellas/Short Stories

Watched (novella)

Corey Island (novella, February 2021)

Young Adult and Middle Grade

Secrets of the Ambassadors (MG)

Mysterious Pirates of the Pacific (MG)

Running Down a Dream (YA)

Boonville (YA, Book 1, January 2021)